SELECTED STORIES

JAKE KERR

QUANTA

10 9 8 7 6 5 4 3 2

Published by Quanta Books
Dallas, Texas

CONTENTS

FOR MY EDITORS

SELECTED STORIES

The Old Equations

HUGH HOWEY
ON "THE OLD EQUATIONS"

I read this story over lunch at a café in South America, and I was moved nearly to tears. Maybe it's from being on the road a lot the last few years, the challenge of getting a call through to my wife, the fickleness of Skype, but this one really hit close to home.

Perhaps the story is especially poignant for students of physics, who understand what is happening before the characters do, but this is a riveting read for anyone.

Imagination defined the advance of physics in the twentieth century. Although we were enticed by the less challenging models of minor thinkers like Einstein, science reached higher, and the era of quantum mechanics changed civilization. Naturally, very few remember Einstein these days—he died during the First World War, after publishing a widely ignored theory that would have set physics back centuries—and instead our future has been shaped by the models developed by visionaries such as Planck, Schrödinger, and Jain.

Pascal Delacroix, Lucasian Chair of Mathematics, Cambridge, from 500 Years of Physics, Oxford Press, 2187

May 5, 2193

My dearest James,

Surprise!

Yes, the final item on your launch checklist is this special message from me.

I miss you already. But you know that. What you don't know is just how proud I am of you. You were born for this, and no one could possibly be able to handle such a demanding job as well as you. I saw the joy in your eyes when we agreed in your taking the mission. Although I cried and complained, and it seemed like I hated the idea, the reality is that, more than anything, I was and am happy for you. I guess I was just scared—I'm still scared, but I know that this is how our life was meant to be. I'm prepared for it. And proud. Did I mention I'm proud of you?

Know that even while we are millions of miles apart, my heart will always be with you. Ten years is not so long. I'm sad that for most of the journey I won't be able to hear from you, but you'll be able to hear from me, and that's more than some people have, isn't it?

So this is the first of many, many reminders of the person you are leaving back on Earth, and also of the love that you are bringing with you.

I love you so much.

Kate

Jimbo,

Your wife left me like no room to leave a note on this damn page. Incredibly proud of you, man. Jealous, too, you lucky bastard! I told Marsden to let me hit you with news from home, but he said no dice. Short messages from control and your wife only. Guess you won't know the winner of the next ten Super Bowls until you get home, as your wife sure as hell won't be mentioning it! Anyway, going to miss you, man. I'll keep the beer cold.

Tony

_____

May 6, 2193—E-LC transmission

14:23:31: Testy test test test. askdfjowig. Yeah, this is a fucking test.

14:23:58: Sorry about that, Colonel. All systems are working perfectly on our end. First sail calibration is still set for 4 June. General Marsden wants us to get through a few more days of testing the QE comlink, so you won't hear from your wife as soon as you may like, but don't be alarmed. Just to clarify, because you seemed concerned before liftoff—we're still planning on sticking to the original schedule of odd days being hers and even days ours. Marsden made it very clear that we're not to take any of your personal message time unless it was critical. Thought you'd like to hear that. Smitty [MESSAGE TRANSMITTED]

May 9, 2193—E-LC transmission

18:03:32: James, it's me. Kate. Wow, this is so weird. I'm writing to you, and you're out there in space. Sorry I haven't written, but General Marsden wanted to get all the systems with the sail and monitors and stuff perfect first. I guess I'm glad that he's using the word "perfect." It makes me worry a little less.

I told Tony that it must be beautiful to watch the planets float by, and he laughed and said you are basically encased in lead with no windows. You never told me that. You made it sound so romantic, and now it sounds oppressive. I hope that you are able to keep that sparkle in your eyes for the whole trip, despite the conditions. It was always there whenever you looked in the sky. Remember that, James. Whenever things get tough, remember me holding your hand as you looked up at the sky, the stars reflecting in your eyes.

It's only been a few days, and I can't wait to hear from you on the fourth. Don't worry—I can handle ten years, as long as I can hear from you. I'm running out of space. Love you so very mu [WARNING: CHARACTER LIMIT REACHED—MESSAGE TRANSMITTED]

May 23, 2193—E-LC transmission

18:02:18: Sorry I didn't write last time. It is awful that I'm only allowed to sit down at 6 and can only write a few paragraphs every other day. Anyway, I shouldn't use the space to complain! Amy had a performance at school at 4:30, and your sister would have killed me if I missed it. I couldn't get to the base until almost 7 because of traffic. General Marsden said I couldn't even send you an "I love you," and he wouldn't give me a make-up day. Sometimes I hate the stick up his ass, but then I remember that it's one of the things helping keep you alive, so I try to be thankful.

Anyway, I'm very excited that I'll be able to get a message from you soon, but General stick-up-his-ass (kidding!) says not to expect more than a few words as this is your first time setting up your comlink. Still, even a few words will be a blessing. I miss you horribly, and it's only been three weeks. Ten years seems almost unbearable now. Sorry to be such a downer. I'm sure I'll feel better after I hear from you next week.

Love, ~Kate [MESSAGE TRANSMITTED]

———————————————

June 4, 2193—E-LC transmission

12:03:01: Jim, it's Mars. Did the sail calibrate? Were you able to initiate the quantum link? I'll assume you're having some com problems. Let us know what went wrong with the process when you get the link established. [MESSAGE TRANSMITTED]

15:32:54: Jim, are you okay? We're still waiting to hear from you. I'm going to kill Ollie if he didn't account for something on your quantum pair. I'll be up until we hear from you. We don't want to stress our QE link with too many messages, so don't make me keep hassling you, soldier. [MESSAGE TRANS-MITTED]

19:02:17: Jim, I'm going to go against all of my instincts and assume the best. I'm working from the theory that you didn't have time to get the link initiated with calibration going on. Understandable. I'm hoping for the best next month. I'll tell everyone that it was a communication issue and that everything is fine. Don't fuck-ing make a liar out of me or I'll kick your ass. Mars [MESSAGE TRANSMITTED]

June 4, 2193—LC-E transmission

12:42:12: Hello? I sure hope to hell this thing is working. What the fuck is happening back on Earth? Why are you sending messages at all hours? Half of them don't even make sense. I thought you were going to do one message a day at 18:00? Why are you guys so worried about this calibration? It's going perfectly. This isn't Tony fooling around is it? I can't believe Mars would let him do that. Je-sus. Someone better answer. [MESSAGE RECEIVED]

June 4, 2193—E-LC transmission

19:59:33: Colonel, this is Smitty. General Marsden and your wife have already left. You're almost eight hours late. What happened? We can't send through any more messages due to the strain on the QE link, so we'll have to catch up next calibration. Just give us a status update, and we'll figure it out next time. [MESSAGE TRANSMITTED]

June 4, 2193—LC-E transmission

12:43:41: What the hell are you talking about Smitty? I'm 43 minutes late, which is within the range we considered as acceptable before I left. I'm looking at the clock right now. Shit, I don't want to wait another month to talk to Kate. Can't believe you guys fucked this up on our very first calibration.

Anyway, all readings are normal except for distance traveled. It's off slightly. I'll have more data for the next calibration. Just don't fuck it up next time, and make sure Kate is there. [MESSAGE RECEIVED

June 7, 2193—E-LC transmission

18:00:04: I am so mad, but I'm not sure if I should be mad at you or the idiots who planned this mission. How could it take you so long to set up the quantum link? This is killing me, and now I have to wait another month. Argh! At least you're okay. I was so scared when they said something was wrong and I missed you, but General Marsden was so calm and kind. Tony told me that sometimes that even though the buttons are shiny or new it doesn't mean they don't occasionally get stuck. I laughed, but I'm not sure that it made me feel better.

Ugh, here I am venting at you again, and you're the one who's all alone in space. Sorry! I am so proud of you, and I love you.

Oh, I'm supposed to tell you that your Uncle Bill broke his leg skateboarding. Your dad said you'd laugh at that. Everyone here wants me to pass along messages and stories. I'm watching your friends and family share their life with me. It makes me feel closer to you, James, even though you are so far away. I love you so much. Please make sure that everything is [WARNING: CHARACTER LIMIT REACHED—MESSAGE TRANSMITTED]

June 16, 2193—E-LC transmission

12:03:34: Colonel, you need to make sure the comlink is set up by 16:00:00. Not to put any pressure on you, but it's so the President can talk to you. General Marsden will have more details later. Oh, and a reminder, Kate's scheduled session tomorrow was kicked by General Marsden so we can send you the latest data points on the sail calibration. You'll hear from her on 19 June and then we pick up the normal schedule. Smitty [MESSAGE TRANSMITTED]

June 22, 2193—E-LC transmission

18:01:33: Jim, it's Mars. The President wants to communicate with you on the next sail calibration. Yeah, I'm sure you noticed it's the fourth of July, and yes it means you won't be able to send a message to Kate. You wanted to be the hero? Well, look here—you're the hero. Anyway, just be your normal "oh golly" humble self. It's one of the things that I hate about you but everyone seems to find endearing, so you have my permission to be yourself. Just this once.

Not sure what Kate is saying, as I've forbidden anyone from accessing her logs. Whatever you say is between you and her. I just wanted to say that she's being a real trooper. Seems strong. Pissed as all hell about the com issues, but I can't blame her. Anyway, she seems okay. Shit, I don't know about women, dammit. All I'm trying to say is that you shouldn't worry about her. [MESSAGE TRANSMITTED]

June 23, 2193—E-LC transmission

18:00:41: Well, they finally told me, and I'm both proud and angry. Mostly angry, to be honest. I can't stand that I'll have to wait another month to hear from you because you'll be talking to the president. Of course it IS the president, which is a bit overwhelming. I have to admit that I'm getting quite a bit of attention over your mission, and now the president is going to talk to my James on the fourth of July because he's a hero and inspiration. Is it bad that I'm kind of thrilled that I'm being asked to do talk shows? I know that sounds so shallow, but talking about you to others makes you feel closer somehow. Ha, that almost sounds like I'm rationalizing this celebrity thing, but honestly it's not. If I can't talk to you, I can at least talk ABOUT you.

I was invited to dinner by Tony and Gwen this evening. They'll ask about you, and I don't know what I'll say. Because I don't know. But it's nice that they ask. They care, you know?

I'm still angry about not talking to you. Maybe if I ask the President he'll say s [WARNING: CHARACTER LIMIT REACHED—MESSAGE TRANSMITTED]

July 3, 2193—E-LC transmission

17:59:44: M. says I only have 50 characters. Love you! ~Kate

18:03:07: Colonel, all systems are fine on our end. I sure hope you can get the comlink initiated tomorrow. We finally got all the data from your first missed broadcast, and the only issue was the slight calibration error on distance. Beyond that things look good. The systems on the ship haven't so much as hiccupped. Just make sure you get that communication link set up ASAP. Smitty [MESSAGE TRANSMITTED]

July 4, 2193—E-LC transmission

15:21:21: Jim, please tell me you'll have the comlink set up soon. I'm forbidding anyone from coming near the com station until I hear from you. You know what to do, soldier! Mars [MESSAGE TRANSMITTED]

15:44:03: Jim, we just checked every fucking scan, transmission, assessment, and data point, and everything looks normal. Please get on the line within the next 15 minutes. I told the president that it would probably be good to wait, but he's adamant. He wants to go live with you at 16:00. LIVE. Mars [MESSAGE TRANSMITTED]

16:00:00: Colonel Murphy, this is President Wallace. I just wanted to say how proud we are of you. You embody the true American spirit! [MESSAGE TRANSMITTED]

16:00:12: They are telling me that there may be sunspots affecting our conversation, and that I may not get a response from you. How unfortunate, I was hoping to hear how beautiful space must be as you fly past at such extraordinary speed. I wonder if you see out your window what we think of when we think of America—truth and beauty quickly passing us by as we look forward to an even better future. But we should stop and enjoy the view, don't you think Colonel? [MESSAGE TRANSMITTED]

16:00:41: I'm sure your view is beautiful. [MESSAGE TRANSMITTED]

16:00:47: It is unfortunate we can't hear of it due to the sun. Perhaps next time, Colonel. Remember, all of America is proud of you. God bless you, and God bless America. [MESSAGE TRANSMITTED]

16:23:28: Jim, I'm cutting the link for today, but I'll have Smitty monitor the line in case we hear from you. Don't expect to hear from Kate for a few days. All the messages today put a strain on the quantum link. Sorry. Mars. [MESSAGE TRANSMITTED]

July 5, 2193—E-LC transmission

18:06:18: Colonel, I don't know if you're there, but we're seeing normal readings across the board. General Marsden has everyone believing in the sunspots story, but what is really going on? We're returning to the normal com schedule on 7 July. You'll hear from Kate then. Smitty [MESSAGE TRANSMITTED]

July 6, 2193—E-LC transmission

18:01:08: Jim, I fear the worst, but I'm not against giving everyone one more month of hope. Hell, I need another month of hope. Readings are normal, so there is that. I expect this is your ineptitude and not anything worse. I'll forgive ineptitude this once. Just don't let it happen in August. Please. Mars. [MESSAGE TRANSMITTED]

———————————

July 7, 2193—E-LC transmission

17:59:32: Dearest James, I am so sorry you haven't heard from me. General Marsden wouldn't let me talk to you until the sunspot interference died down. He said you wouldn't even get the messages. I guess I yelled a bit, but he put his foot down. Sometimes I hate that man. But don't worry, I'm okay. I was just so worried. Not hearing from you is killing me inside. First it's normal first run mistakes, and now it's sunspots. I haven't heard from you in over two months!

Please please please tell me you're okay, and you'll be able to talk to me soon? Please? I know you're okay. I just want to hear it. I love you. ~Kate [MESSAGE TRANSMITTED]

———————————

July 4, 2193—LC-E transmission

12:33:12: Kate, are you there? I just got your message. Is everything okay? I can't make sense of half of what you are saying to me, and I'm now getting a couple messages a day. Have you guys changed the schedule? [MESSAGE RECEIVED]

July 7, 2193—E-LC transmission

19:03:28: Holy shit, Colonel, am I glad to hear from you! It's Smitty. We've been worried sick. What happened on 4 July, and why are you contacting us now? The next calibration is weeks away. Is something wrong? [MESSAGE TRANSMITTED]

July 4, 2193—LC-E transmission

12:35:22: Smitty, I have no idea what you are talking about. The calibration is going on right now. How could I have missed it? [MESSAGE RECEIVED]

12:57:22: Smitty, you there? I only have a few hours before I need to shut down. Where's Kate? [MESSAGE RECEIVED]

July 7, 2193—E-LC transmission

19:53:47: Jim, it's Mars. Sorry I took so long. I have communications locked down due to all these issues, and it took me a while to get here. I just went over the logs, and I am completely lost. Are you saying it's 4 July right now? [MESSAGE TRANSMITTED]

July 4, 2193—LC-E transmission

13:23:11: Mars, I'm not in the mood for jokes. I'm looking at the computer screen right now, and it's 4 July. What the hell are you guys up to? Can you get Kate on the line? [MESSAGE RECEIVED]

July 7, 2193—E-LC transmission

19:54:53: I'll get Kate on the line at ASAP, but right now I need to figure this out. What's your location? [MESSAGE TRANSMITTED]

July 4, 2193—LC-E transmission

13:24:02: That's what I can't understand, Mars. The instruments don't match up. Acceleration is perfect—constant since launch, but I've covered even more distance than the revisions from the last calibration, and way more than our initial estimates. Just checked it three times. Something's out of whack. And now the clock thing is getting worse. I know there were some unknowns, but this is fucked up beyond all belief. And why is the message frequency now several times a day? With the augmentation to handle the G forces Archer said to expect some disorientation, but this is ridiculous. Hell, I FEEL perfectly normal. [MESSAGE RECEIVED]

July 7, 2193—E-LC transmission

19:57:01: I don't know, Jim. We need more time to figure this out. Let me get the guys on it until the next calibration. Maybe you went through a particle field or something else we don't know about, and it has affected some instruments and your perceptions. Look, we can't stress the QE link any more. Every time we exchange multiple messages, it becomes unstable. I'll tell Kate we got a short update from you, but let's not let her know there are any problems. I don't want to worry you, but she's been extremely tense after missing the first two comlinks.

I'm just glad you're okay. [MESSAGE TRANSMITTED]

August 3, 2193—E-LC transmission

19:54:33: James, Mars is making me leave, so if you get the link set up make him get me. MAKE HIM. I NEED to hear from you. I understand that there is something wrong with your instruments or something, so I don't blame you. But you MUST be here for the September calibration. I desperately miss you. I love you so much. ~Kate [MESSAGE TRANSMITTED]

August 3, 2193—LC-E transmission

13:14:20: Smitty, you there? We clearly have major problems, but that can wait. Get Kate. [MESSAGE RECEIVED]

August 14, 2193—E-LC transmission

02:44:04: Colonel, this is Davis. It's 3 AM here and everyone is asleep. But don't worry. General Marsden made it clear—if you contacted us the first call was to your wife and the next one was to him. We'll get her here for you, sir.

04:08:44: James, are you there? I've missed you so much! I can't believe I get to hear from you early! General Marsden says we only have a couple of exchanges, so I'll just say a few words and then let you speak. Oh God, how I've missed your voice—seeing your words. Are you getting my messages? Are you okay? Can I do anything for you?

Please respond quickly. [MESSAGE TRANSMITTED]

August 3, 2193—LC-E transmission

14:39:23: Kate, I'm here. I love you and miss you, too. More than you can possibly imagine. Yes, I've gotten every single one of your wonderful, maddening, crazy, loving messages. I love that Tony and Gwen are expecting. I love that you hate Mars one day and appreciate him the next. (I'm the same way, as if you didn't know that). I love that on some days you tell me the most wonderful details of your life—our life—and other days you just vent.

I'm fine. I'm perfectly fine, and everything is perfect on this amazing ship. The worst part is being without you and our friends, but other than that I just have to deal with boredom. Being alone can be hard. I can't deny that. But this is all just temporary. We're already past a chunk of time. Nine or ten years still seems monumentally long. I know that. But it's not so long that we'll miss our lives together. When I get back you'll be 38, and I'll be 40. We can still have kids. We can run off to Venice or just sleep in and watch TV.

I wish I had more to say, but you know me—I've never [MESSAGE RECEIVED]

14:46:02: Dammit. I hate the character limits on this quantum shit. Anyway, I was going to say that I've never been one for lots of talking and here I am running out of characters. I guess I will need to figure this out if we're only going to talk every 30 days.

I love you, Kate. I miss you. James [MESSAGE RECEIVED]

August 14, 2193—E-LC transmission

04:23:38: I'm crying, James. Damn you, you made me cry and Smith and General Marsden will be in here soon. I hate when people see me cry!

I love you so much. ~Kate [MESSAGE TRANSMITTED]

August 14, 2193—E-LC transmission

04:32:42: Jim, it's Mars. We've pulled in every analyst and expert we could find. It turns out the initial thought of this being due to an astronomical anomaly isn't possible. We had both engineers and statisticians go through the cosmological data, and there is nothing out of the ordinary. I mean nothing. We did confirm your assessment. One or more of your gauges is out of calibration. That could also account for some of your disorientation.

With that in mind I need to gather more data from you in terms of your perceptions the next time we have a link. Honestly, I'd like to peg you as crazy and call it a day, but with gauges out of calibration you could be right. Maybe we're the crazy ones. [MESSAGE TRANSMITTED]

August 16, 2193—E-LC transmission

16:32:44: Colonel, we almost lost the QE link on 14 August. We're still working out the limits, but it looks like we're going to have to hold the monthly exchanges to 2 incoming/2 outgoing. General Marsden says this will give you one exchange with your wife and one for us. It's not a lot, but the quantum entanglement is very unstable. We can't risk breaking the connection. Next message coming 19 August. Smitty [MESSAGE TRANSMITTED]

September 2, 2193—E-LC transmission

12:02:33: Colonel, it's Smitty. Did you get the link set up? We're hoping you got your ship clocks calibrated correctly during the last link. I'm standing by. [MESSAGE TRANSMITTED]

September 3, 2193—E-LC transmission

18:00:04: I hate sunspots! I'm so depressed. All I want to do is see your words. Your words! How hard is that? They said you would be able to talk to me every month, and here it is month four, and I've heard from you once. ONCE! I tried to get General Marsden to maybe see about setting up the comlink next week instead of the long wait. I even told him I'd swap two weeks of sending messages just to hear from you, but he wouldn't even consider it.

I don't know what to do, James. I feel so powerless. I live and speak to you in the vacuum of space, and then—nothing. [MESSAGE TRANSMITTED]

September 4, 2193—E-LC transmission

18:18:14: Jim, it's Mars. I was afraid you wouldn't hook up with us on 2 September, but I'm not surprised. All of us are pretty much just waiting until we hear from you, whenever that is. I'm still not telling Kate that we have some kind of unknown problem, but I'm sure she's already covered that with you multiple times. Needless to say, I'm not her favorite person in the world right now.

I'm assuming that we have a few weeks until we get a link. The physicists want me to ask you to keep very close track of our incoming messages. We need you to log them in the computer and stamp them with your arrival time. Have that handy when we talk. I'll have Doctor Singh with me next time, and he'll be asking you about the variations between our time stamps and yours. [MESSAGE TRANSMITTED]

September 5, 2193—E-LC transmission

18:02:32: I'm so sorry about the other day. I NEVER feel like I'm not talking to you, especially after what you said last month. I was just sad and frustrated and not having the best day. I saw Jackie Merriweather holding hands with her new boyfriend, and it made me so intensely jealous. And then I can't talk to you, so not only can't I hold your hand, I can't even read your words.

I'm thinking this is one of those venting messages, so I should just sign off. Why did we ever agree to this?

I do love you so very much. ~Kate [MESSAGE TRANSMITTED]

September 13, 2193—E-LC transmission

18:02:02: Happy thirtieth birthday, my love. We had a celebration at the house, and your dad flew in from Phoenix. Isn't that great? We thought rehabilitation would take months, but there he was. We let him blow out your candles. He blew out every single one, although he coughed a bit at the end. He laughed and said that he may not be as strong as he once was, but he'd live long enough to see his son return from Gliese 581 d! Isn't that great?

I read your message at the party. It's the first time I've shared it with anyone. I've been kind of keeping it to myself as my special thing, but the time seemed right to share it with others. Your words didn't leave many dry eyes. Tony said to bank on the sleeping in and watching TV more than Venice, which got a laugh.

I'm getting nervous about October 2, but I'm starting to understand that space travel is something you simply can't predict. As General Marsden says—there are just so many variables. Still, please be there. Love, ~Kate [MESSAGE TRANSMITTED]

September 2, 2193—LC-E transmission

15:58:13: Anyone there? Of all times to have shit get messed up, it has to be now. Not sure what your time stamp shows, but I'm four hours behind schedule on getting the link up. Sail calibration is almost done, so we have to talk fast. Smitty? [MESSAGE RECEIVED]

September 29, 2193—E-LC transmission

17:13:23: Jim, it's Mars. Thank God you're safe. I almost gave up hope when you missed the 2 September calibration and link.

We need to get this problem solved. Do you have the time stamps? I'm calling for Professor Singh. Hopefully he's nearby. He needs to know how closely they match up. [MESSAGE TRANSMITTED]

September 2, 2193—LC-E transmission

16:09:58: Christ, this is fucked up. Anyway, I have the time stamps. They show incoming at increasing intervals. They started at one per day and are now coming in at nearly twice a day. I also followed up on the doctor's recommendations and logged my sleep cycle and have done daily cognitive tests. Normal across the board.

Is Kate there? [MESSAGE RECEIVED]

September 29, 2193—E-LC transmission

17:58:55: Colonel Murphy, this is Doctor Singh. Are the time differences random or is there some kind of order to them? Do you have any other things that appear to be out of phase? Also, can you remember feeling any anomalies? It may even be as slight as a flash in your eyes or a tingle on your skin.

Jim, it's Mars. Kate's in the other room. I'll bring her in after you send your answers to Doctor Singh. [MESSAGE TRANSMITTED]

September 2, 2193—LC-E transmission

16:46:09: Hard to tell, Doc. The times appear random, but when I look at them as a whole, they appear to be slowly increasing in frequency. And, yes, the whole fucking flight appears to be out-of-phase. I'm somehow covering more distance without our acceleration calculations being off. I'm starting to think I'm going crazy, because there have been no flashes and no tingling. Nothing like that. Beyond the bizarre data we're seeing this trip couldn't be more normal. I guess that's good for Ollie and his team, but it makes for frustrating troubleshooting. [MESSAGE RECEIVED]

September 29, 2193—E-LC transmission

18:04:49: James, what is happening??? I haven't heard from you in almost two months! Is everything okay? I'm so afraid for you, James.

General Marsden said you only have a few minutes. I could kill him for making me wait nearly all this time and then telling me you only have a few minutes. I want to hear hours of your thoughts, your dreams, and your words, but I get just minutes. I'll shut up. Please just let me see your words and imagine your voice as you tell me you're okay. Please. Quickly. Please. [MESSAGE TRANSMITTED]

September 2, 2193—LC-E transmission

16:51:12: I have just a few moments, but it's not Mars' fault. I couldn't get the comlink initiated until it was four hours late. I loved your birthday message. I must say that Tony was wrong—after ten years apart, I can drag my ass out of bed for a trip to Venice.

You know, I figured the one thing that what would keep me going would be your messages. But now that there have been problems I realize that I want—I need—to have you see MY messages, too. It's the only way I can make sure you know I exist.

I think of you constantly. I think of our past, and I think of our future. I like to think of the more mature, elegant, and beautiful woman who will be waiting for me when I return. Of course, here is where you ask why you aren't elegant, mature, or beautiful now, and I don't have an answer for that, because you are.

I guess the point is that I want to remind you that I think of our future. That's what gets me through the day—your messages from the present, and my dreams for our future.

I need to go. I have so much I want [MESSAGE RECEIVED]

December 12, 2193—E-LC transmission

18:32:13: Jim, it's Mars. I'm sorry for all the dead ends, but I think we've found something. One of the physicists in Bern remembers a crackpot theoretical physicist from 200 years ago named Albert Einstein. He was an amateur who died during World War One after publishing a handful of theories that no one took seriously. The thing is that they kind of match what we're seeing here. On the extremely off chance that this guy was actually right, we're looking into it.

It's something, at least.

He just gave me the briefing this afternoon, and I don't understand 90% of it. I'll have him dumb it down even more and then I'll explain it to you in the next uplink. [MESSAGE TRANSMITTED]

December 14, 2193—E-LC transmission

18:11:28: Jim, it's Mars. The physicists are actually excited about this Einstein lead. I still can't understand half of it, but the essence is that time is not a constant, it's relative to the speed of light, which is the actual constant. What this means is that the faster you travel and the closer you get to the speed of light, the slower time goes for you.

Okay, here's the kicker, and here is what is getting all the brainiacs excited. His theory basically says that as you are increasing in speed, time will slow down by a specific ratio, and that's what we're seeing with the messages. We have a ton more calculations to run through, and no one is sure how this integrates with quantum physics, but CERN is saying they are going to do some practical tests on this crazy theory, but it looks like the crackpot could actually have been a genius.

This is going to be difficult to grasp, but I want you to think long and hard about what this means for you. I won't say more than that. I'll have more later. [MESSAGE TRANSMITTED]

December 16, 2193—E-LC transmission

18:08:00: Jim, it's Mars. The scientists didn't screw around. Every test they ran confirmed Einstein's theory. Hell, you're a living confirmation of the theory. I hope you did what I asked and thought about this, because the scenario is not good, buddy.

All our calculations anticipated you passing the speed of light to make this trip in ten years. You will not pass the speed of light. You will approach it, but you won't be able to go faster. Einstein figured it out, and CERN just confirmed it. It's impossible. I can't be more blunt than this, Jim: Your mission will now take 41 years from our perspective.

Okay, that's not all. You mentioned how you are covering more ground than you expected, and you've seen these messages come to you faster and faster. That's because space is warping at the speed you are traveling. I still can't believe this, but here's the kicker: From your perspective, the trip will take only 5 years. As I said, time is slowing down for you.

This has a dramatic impact on this project, but it also h [WARNING: CHARACTER LIMIT REACHED—MESSAGE TRANSMITTED]

18:14:47: I'm going to risk another transmission, because this is so important. Jim, this has a dramatic impact not just on the mission but you personally. When you arrive back on Earth, it will be 5 years from now for you, but we'll all be 41 years older. I'm so sorry.

I'm going to let Kate know over breakfast tomorrow. She'll have plenty of time before your transmission, which should be in a few weeks. Mars [MESSAGE TRANSMITTED]

———————————

December 17, 2193—E-LC transmission

18:00:44: General Marsden told me.

I spent all day thinking about it, and I think it's a load of shit. Time has no meaning? Space can be stretched? I asked questions. Lots and lots of questions, James. And the scientists all give me the same answers, but their answers don't scream "time dilation" (which is what they're calling it) to me. They scream "someone fucked up and is covering their ass."

Sorry. I just am very frustrated on your behalf. Don't worry, I'll push and push until we see something that makes sense.

There is absolutely no way that I'm not going to see you for forty years. [MESSAGE TRANSMITTED]

———

December 21, 2193—E-LC transmission

18:03:01: James, I did some research on this Einstein fellow. Did you know that he died before quantum physics? The core branch of science for the past 200 years, and this crazy guy didn't even consider it. THIS is who we are looking to for guidance on a communication issue?

Also, Doctor Singh told me that they still have no idea how our quantum link is working across space and time. He actually told me that you are a "quantum reference point," and so you are talking to us in the future. After hearing that, how can we take them seriously? You know me, James. I'll dig and claw and fight until I get the truth.

I know you're okay, but someone messed up something, and I'll find out. Next link let's skip the personal stuff and get to the bottom of the problem. You're right there and probably know what's going on. We can solve this even if the scientists can't.

Your father called, but I haven't had time to call him back. At your birthday party, he asked if he could talk with you, but I'm not sure General Marsden would allow i [WARNING: CHARACTER LIMIT REACHED—MESSAGE TRANSMITTED]

———————————

October 2, 2193—LC-E transmission

12:44:39: Smitty, this is Colonel Murphy. Link is set up. I want you to get Kate on the line ASAP. [MESSAGE RECEIVED]

December 26, 2193—E-LC transmission

14:48:12: Colonel, this is Smitty. Glad to hear from you. I'm going to get General Marsden. Hold tight.

15:13:59: Jim, it's Mars. Kate is here, but first I'm handing control over to Doctor Archer. She knows she has only one transmission, so pay attention to every word.

15:14:19: Colonel, your initial assessment was for a 10 year mission. While that is now shorter for you, the circumstances on Earth have changed radically. Your expectations on return have to be completely altered. I have confidence that you will be able to handle the strain, but I need you to be honest with us and honest with yourself. Please share any fears, concerns, or other psychological problems or issues you are facing, no matter how small. We will do our best to provide for them, even with this difficult means of communication.

Be strong. But be honest with yourself. When you return, you are not going to see the wife, family, or friends you expect. Some may not be alive. Colonel, I handled your initial screening, and I know you can handle this challenge. [MESSAGE TRANSMITTED]

October 2, 2193—LC-E transmission

13:11:39: No shit, doc. Put Kate on. [MESSAGE RECEIVED]

December 26, 2193—E-LC transmission

15:15:45: James, I have missed you so much! I have nothing to say. You've seen my words for months, and I've seen nothing from you, so please just tell me you're okay! [MESSAGE TRANSMITTED]

October 2, 2193—LC-E transmission

13:12:00: Kate, I'm perfectly fine, but please pay attention to this very carefully. I know you don't believe it, but you must. They explained the theory behind the old equations that the physicists are discussing, and while they are strange, the concepts are clear and make sense. I'm so sorry, Kate, but this is how things are. I don't want them to be, but they are. Trust me. Relativity is real. I can't go faster than the speed of light. Time dilation is real. All of it is real. I see it every day. Every day I receive multiple messages from Earth. It is wonderful to have the constant communication, but it is sad to watch time fly by.

Please believe me. It is much better for us to talk about our new plans and how we are going to deal with that than pretending it isn't real. I love you so much that the last thing I want to do is hurt you, and I know this is probably hurting you. But we can get past this.

We cannot be sad. We cannot be angry. We need to just find a way to deal with what life has dealt us. We WILL see each [MESSAGE RECEIVED]

13:06:44 : We will see each other again, my love. Talk to Doctor Archer or Mars. They can give you perspective. Mars told me that I can't reply more than twice due to lack of stability of the quantum entanglement, but this is important, Kate. Let's not look at the problems. Let's look ahead at the answers. [MESSAGE RECEIVED]

———————————

December 31, 2193—E-LC transmission

18:01:03: James, I don't want you to worry. I was being selfish and I let my emotions get in the way of thinking clearly. I spent a long time talking to General Marsden, and I understand time dilation now. You know me—I'm not one to just sit back and give up. Don't be mad, but I asked him about abandoning the mission. He wouldn't even consider it. I don't want to belabor the point, because I know you won't agree, but I really think that with everything all screwed up that they should turn you around and bring you home.

Anyway, maybe he told you, but if not—that isn't going to happen.

Believe me, James, I am thinking. Maybe they can send another ship that I can be on to join you? It's not that crazy. Maybe we could live on Gliese 581 d as the first colonists. They've done husband and wife missions before, right? God, 41 years is so long. That's longer than I've been alive! I'm sorry. I know it is hard for you, too. But will you love me when I'm old? Will you even know me? I'm sorry. Happy New Year, my love, although I k [WARNING: CHARACTER LIMIT REACHED – MESSAGE TRANSMITTED]

————————————————

January 17, 2194—E-LC transmission

18:00:03: James, Gwen had her baby. They named him James after you, and they asked us to be his godparents. I think that is really nice.

I'm still meeting with Doctor Archer. She helps a lot, but it is still difficult. The press has found out about what is happening, and they are calling me constantly. The headlines are all about how when you finally return, you'll be 35, and I'll be almost 70.

It's hard.

Tony joked that when you return your godson will be older than you, and I started crying and couldn't stop. I know he felt terrible, but I wanted to just kill him.

Will you still love me when I'm old and gray, and you're still young and handsome?

I have to go. [MESSAGE TRANSMITTED]

———————————————

November 1, 2193—LC-E transmission

12:14:23: Smitty, link is established. I'll wait on instructions. Please make sure Kate is there. [MESSAGE RECEIVED]

February 10, 2194 E-LC transmission

21:32:01: Jim, it's Mars. Great to hear from you. Listen: You really need to get to Kate. I'm very worried about her. She won't tell me what's wrong, but I'm sure it's finally dawning on her that she won't see you for 40 years. She's shut out Archer, too, and they had been talking regularly. If you need to, send a double transmission this once. You know that I need you both strong. I'm going to clear the message buffer. Wait for her message and then reply. [MESSAGE TRANSMITTED]

12:45:03: James, I am so sorry to tell you this, but your father passed away. We've kept it very quiet because the press is still looking for every possible angle to write about you. They are horrible.

He died in his sleep. Maybe it was for the best, he was fighting so hard.

All I want to do is hold you and make you feel better, my love. I am so sorry. I feel like the weight of the world is on my shoulders. I need to be strong for you and everyone around me. But I don't know if I can handle it. It's hard, James.

And then I think of you and feel guilty. So guilty.

I was at the funeral, and as they lowered your dad's casket in the ground, I couldn't help but think that it was like your ship. A metal casket taking you to some unknown beyond. I know that's grim and sad and not true because I know I'll see you again, but it won't be for so long. [MESSAGE TRANSMITTED]

November 1, 2193—LC-E transmission

13:50:01: Kate, please don't let everything overwhelm you. I am so thankful that you told me about Dad. To be very clear—I never expected to see him again. I know that sounds harsh, and I know he's a tough old bird, but even he knew that his cancer wasn't going to give him much time. We said our goodbyes.

I committed my life to this mission. I knew I'd have to leave my life behind and that things would be different when I returned.

This is so hard, because I will be responding to messages I've just seen that you sent weeks ago. So bear with me if you can't remember what I'm talking about.

Yes, I will still find you beautiful. Yes, I will still want to feel you against me as we fall asleep. Yes, I will kiss you with the same passion as when I left, if not more. Yes, I will be there for you always.

Never doubt me, Kate. I don't doubt you. [MESSAGE RECEIVED]

February 10, 2194—E-LC transmission

12:57:56: I will be strong, James. How sad is this—I'm safe on Earth, and you're in a dangerous ship sailing to an unknown planet in a far away solar system, and you're trying to make me feel better. And you just lost your father. I'm ashamed. Mars said I had this one extra message and to make it count, but I don't know what to say other than you inspire me, James. I miss you. ~Kate [MESSAGE TRANSMITTED]

December 1, 2193—LC-E transmission

11:44:32: Smitty, Mars? What is going on? The messages have started to slow down. Is there something wrong? Everything is fine here. I'd wish you Happy Thanksgiving, but you've already celebrated Christmas and New Years. Still no problems on my end. Just a bit worried about you guys, actually. [MESSAGE RECEIVED]

May 19, 2194—E-LC transmission

16:58:54: Jim, it's Mars. I've been waiting to hear from you before giving you the bad news. As you've noticed, the QE link has become unstable. We're not sure if it'll hold up. We've cut transmission down to the bare minimum in the hope that the entanglement will restore itself, but I have to be honest, buddy. It doesn't look good. I don't know how many more messages we have, but we will most likely lose our link soon.

17:07:32: James, it's Kate. I haven't heard from you in over 3 months, but I just want you to know I'm not worried. Smitty told me we've seen instability in the link before, so I'm sure everything is fine. So ignore that and just tell me how your Thanksgiving went. Yes, I remembered!

General Marsden tells me we only have this one transmission, so I'll just say that even if you don't hear from me every day (or 5 times a day!) I'll be with you. Love you so much, ~Kate [MESSAGE TRANSMITTED]

December 1, 2193—LC-E transmission

13:03:54: I don't know what to say, Kate. This is too much to think about. I don't know if I can survive without hearing from you. As you said, they did have instabilities before. I have to be positive. Tell Mars that if he needs anything from me in the way of working on my half of the quantum pair, that I'll do anything—anything—to get it stabilized.

I'm glad you remembered Thanksgiving. I haven't been in space for a full year yet, and already it feels like ages. Hell, it's been even longer for you. Okay, to be positive—tell Tony I'm proud of his promotion. He knows damn well that running the Mars line is the final step before getting a deep space mission, but tell him I mentioned it anyway. I hope to God he never gets a deep space mission, but don't say that—he'll never understand. Can anyone?

We'll figure the com issue out, Kate. Just remember I love you. I'm the luckiest guy in the world. James [MESSAGE RECEIVED]

August 17, 2194—E-LC transmission

18:00:03: They are only giving me one message every month, James. I don't know how often you'll be getting them, but just know that as you wait for my next message I am still thinking of you. I know you're figuring out what's wrong. That's what I love about you. I could always count on you. I'll wait to hear what you have found out, but I have to tell you that General Marsden has told me that we have only a few messages left. He said that the quantum pair are spinning apart or the link is broken or something like that.

At home there isn't much to report. Everyone is just a few months older and a few months wiser. The press are finally leaving me alone. I know I vent at you about them all the time, but they are vultures. Anyway, it's better, thank God.

I don't know what else to say, James. How sad is that? I have only one message a month for you, and I have nothing to say. I guess life goes on. Love you. ~Kate [MESSAGE TRANSMITTED]

———————————————

December 31, 2193—LC-E transmission

11:44:34: Mars, you know what I'm going to say: This is total bullshit. How can you guys fuck up something as simple as the comlink while a sail the size of the moon is working like a charm? Skipping messaging today to do live diagnostics on my transmission quanta. [MESSAGE RECEIVED]

———————————————

September 23, 2194—E-LC transmission

13:04:03: Jim, I understand your anger. I'm so sorry. I got the final report from Ollie. The QE link is slowly breaking apart. How long we have I don't know. The brainiacs are shocked we've kept it up this long. Anyway, we've given up on maintaining our transmission link with the LEWIS & CLARK and are just now trying to give you guidance on keeping your link alive. We don't know if it's the volume of messages, the rate of messages, or time that is breaking the link. Hell, the CERN guys think that it's the distance, our particles are simply moving to a new, stronger entanglement. Anyway, I'm sure you don't give a shit about this.

We are going to keep the link alive until it breaks apart. It may take a long time if we only send one message every few months. No one knows for sure.

Kate is calm. I don't know what you've been saying to her, but keep it up. Everything else is normal. You'll be back on Earth in another 40 years or so. And although I'll be over 100 then, trust me, I'll still able to beat you into shape. Mars [MESSAGE TRANSMITTED]

January 30, 2194—LC-E transmission

12:04:04: Christ, the time difference is hard. Okay, I have some thoughts. I know the QE is untangling, but perhaps we can turn my transmission particle into a two-way link? Hell, just make it transmit from your side. I don't need to talk, I just need to hear from you guys. You don't know how hard it is to wait even a few days for a message.

Can the physicists work on that? I know it's too late for this calibration, but I could spend the next one doing anything they needed me to do.

Mars, I hate to say this, but if that doesn't work, perhaps we could turn the sail around? You know there is an abort plan in place with catastrophic failure. Damn, I can't believe I'm writing that, but we need to get this fixed.

I'm worried about my link, so I'll just add my message to Kate here.

Kate, please don't worry! You know we have two links. Even if the one breaks down, we'll fix the other one. And if that doesn't work, we'll turn this damn ship around. I'm not sailing into fucking space with nothing but a bunch of holos for company. Anyway [MESSAGE RECEIVED]

———————————————

February 19, 2196—E-LC transmission

14:09:11: Jim, it's Mars. My God, it was great to hear from you a few days ago. I'm sorry you haven't heard from us in a long time. I told everyone to hold off and make one last try to get a message to you when you finally contacted us, and it has taken monumental calculations to get this message through. Nothing you are suggesting will work. Once the particles are entangled, we can't make the kind of changes you are suggesting. Just keep your link alive so we can make sure you are okay.

I'm sorry, but this is the last message you'll hear from us until you get back. I never said this, Jim, but you were the son I never had. So just be safe. I don't think anyone else could do what you're doing. I'm incredibly proud of you.

James, it's Kate. I talked to Ollie and he said he can't guarantee that the link won't ever be back for short periods of time. So I will be sending you a message every day. Every day, James. You may never see them, but know they'll be there floating in space. Just my messages to you. I love you and miss [WARNING: CHARACTER LIMIT REACHED—MESSAGE TRANSMITTED]

March 1, 2194—LC-E transmission

12:38:18: I will assume that my messages are going through, even though yours have stopped. So I am going to make this more like a monthly mission log than anything.

Sail calibration is normal. Acceleration is normal. Life support systems are normal. Everything is fucking normal.

I've watched about 40 holos this month. I liked BREAKDOWN. The woman in that reminded me of Kate. I've done some research on physics, but find it just as maddening as I did in college. I examined the abort system, even though Mars was kind enough to ignore my request to abort the mission, but I guess I'm too good a soldier to abort the mission without orders. So I sail on.

Kate, your final message inspired me, but it is so hard to sit here and just wait. And wait. And wait. I've kept the QE link from Earth open, even though nothing ever comes through. Still, I hope. And wait.

And wait.

Not Hurt

"Are you hurt, Bradford Thomas?"

"No, but it's a mess back here. That was a nasty crash. What the hell happened during re-entry?"

"Mechanical error."

"Doesn't surprise me with the tin can they gave us. Why'd you take so long to answer, Ecks? You hurt?"

"Not hurt."

"Good. Let me check the supplies, clean up a bit, and then I'll come up and join you."

"No, Bradford Thomas. Much damage."

"No shit. My head still hurts from the impact. Maybe I can help."

"Dangerous. Stay, Bradford Thomas."

"Is it hull damage? Should I suit up?

"Fixable."

"Well, that's good, because I just realized the suits are up with you."

"Stay."

"Sounds like a plan. Are you sure you're not hurt? Your voice is a little raspy."

"Not hurt."

"Okay. I'll get everything in order down here and check back in a bit."

"Ecks, you there?"

"Busy."

"No problem. Just wanted to let you know that things are cleaned up and stable down here."

"Good."

"Should I still stay put?"

"Stay."

"Ecks, I may be hurt more than I thought. I'm feeling a little woozy."

"You there, Ecks?"

"Busy."

"Something isn't right. I feel light-headed."

"Stay."

"I didn't say I was coming, dammit. I just said I'm a little dizzy. Maybe I hit my head."

"Fixable."

"What are you talking about? I said I think I may have hit my head."

"Stay. Sit."

"I am sitting. Got any other genius advice?"

———————————

"Ecks, I think I blacked out there for a bit. Do you know what's happening?"

"Air unit damaged. Fixable."

"Oh God. No wonder I can barely stand. I'm suffocating, Ecks. You have to fix this now!"

"Fixable. Will direct air to Bradford Thomas."

"You were keeping the air for yourself? You bastard. Send it to me!"

"Not much."

"I don't care. Send it all to me. I'm dying!"

———————————

"You locked the door on me, you alien bastard? Don't deny it. You are locking me in here so that you can have all the air! Dammit. I told them this would happen. Put me on a ship with a cockroach pilot? Sure, first thing he'll do is stab me in the back. You hear that, Ecks? I'm going to get through the door, and then we'll see who has all the air."

"No break door. Fixable. Bradford Thomas has air."

"Screw you! I don't have crap. I can barely stand. You have so much air I can hear you coughing on it. Let me out!"

"Wait, Bradford Thomas."

───────────────

"Ecks. I can't move. I'm dying."

───────────────

"I'm not breathing as hard. Did you fix it?"

"Not fixed. Gave all air."

"I wish you would have done that before. It's not like we can save it. It recycles, you know?"

"Yes."

"Sorry. I still can't stand, and I have a headache."

───────────────

"Are you there, Ecks?"

"Here."

"Almost done?"

"Soon. Fixed."

"You don't sound too good."

"Not hurt."

"I'm not sure I believe you, buddy."

"Rest, Bradford Thomas. Fixable."

"You did it! I just heard the fans hit, and the air is blowing hard. God, I never thought I'd love the taste of filtered air this much."

"Still have a headache, though."

"Ecks, you there? Look, I understand if you're mad. I was out of line. It's just that I wasn't thinking clearly. Not enough oxygen makes you paranoid. So unlock the door, and let's be friends again."

"Damn, I didn't know aliens could pout. I get it. You saved our lives, and I said some things I shouldn't have. I'm sorry. If it makes you feel any better, I still have a headache. Oh, and I'm guessing a rescue ship is, what, six hours out? When it gets here, I'll recommend you for a commendation or whatever they give you guys."

"Ecks? Talk to me buddy."

"Are you hurt?

Requiem in the Key of Prose

KEN LIU
ON "REQUIEM IN THE KEY OF PROSE"

There's a school of science fiction writing that argues that the author's prose should be "transparent." By not drawing attention to itself and remaining unadorned, the prose gets out of the way so that the reader can better be absorbed by the narrative.

As far as writing advice goes, this is perfectly sensible. Relying on fanciful prose to disguise the fact that the story at hand is not really interesting is a fault that editors see far too often in their slush piles. The supposedly "unadorned" style of transparent prose is, of course, nothing of the sort. But by relying on a set of conventions writers and readers have been taught to expect, it does have the virtue of deemphasizing fiction's artifice, which is helpful for many stories.

However, I must admit to also having a soft spot for stories that revel in the nature of their written-ness, that unabashedly draw attention to their crafted artificiality as a collection of words, grammatical units, sentences, paragraphs, that take pleasure in breaking down the fourth wall and pointing out to the reader where the rivets and seams and joints are. When done well, this kind of fiction can function at multiple levels: as a pure story and as metafictional narrative about the art form itself, and these levels can function contrapuntally to create a deeper appreciation for the miraculous act of storytelling.

"Requiem in the Key of Prose" is an excellent example of this type of story, and it has remained one of my favorite pieces by Jake.

Metaphor

There is such a thing as an antifuse. This device is used to maintain the ongoing flow of electricity when there is local failure.

The antifuse works similarly to a fuse in that it is designed to be sacrificed for a specific goal.

But while a fuse is sacrificed to stop electricity from flowing, an antifuse is sacrificed to guarantee that the electricity does not stop.

Personification

As it gasped for breath, the world scrambled to save itself.

Domes sprung up across the globe, built in desperation from whatever was available. Glass and steel were ripped from buildings and vehicles, then repurposed. Massive oxygen-generation arrays were cobbled together from parts found in cars, hospitals, and air conditioning units. Some cities survived. Most did not.

Norfolk, Virginia, survived by scavenging a good portion of its naval shipyard—a massive turbine and propeller from an aircraft carrier, flat sheets of iron and steel from various ships, oxygen-generating material from submarines. Norfolk's finished oxygen generator was a single massive unit that moved so much air that it was the only city remaining on Earth where you could feel a breeze.

Foreshadowing

Adam couldn't afford to be late for class again. Offering apologies as he went, he shoved his way past the line of students and grabbed a granola bar. Turning to head to the cafeteria register, he ran straight into a girl, sending her tray of food crashing to the floor. His first thought was to apologize and then let her deal with the mess, but one glance changed everything. Her angry pout, her short disheveled hair, the tilt of her hips—everything about her stopped him in his tracks.

He dragged his attention away from her and looked at the clock on the wall over the exit. He had to go or he could pretty much give up any hope of passing the class—and if he didn't, he wouldn't graduate. But as he glanced back at her, thoughts of his future fell by the wayside. She just stood there and looked at him, waiting.

He smiled and then shrugged. "Accidents happen," was all he said before he grabbed her tray, knelt down, and started to help her clean up the mess. She crossed her arms and watched him do all the work.

He did most of the talking, but she didn't seem to mind. He lifted a piece of lettuce off her blouse, and his heart leapt as she finally smiled at him. She said her name was Violet, and he replied by saying he would be joining her for lunch. She didn't say yes, but he didn't care, because she didn't say no either.

The class he couldn't afford to miss had ended by the time their lunch was over. Adam had given up his entire future for her. As he walked to his dorm from the cafeteria, all he could think about was how glad he was that he had.

Passive Voice

Violet was overwhelmed by Adam the first time they met.

She was lost in his beautiful blue eyes, his impossibly black hair, and his smile. More than anything, it was his smile that took her breath away.

When he bumped into her at the cafeteria, she was annoyed until she caught his look. It was apologetic and mischievous and utterly charming. She had asked him several times since that day if he had meant to run into her, and his reply was always ambiguous.

She accepted that.

He was a force that she was just happy to have in her life. He loved her. She never doubted that. But they lived in two different worlds, and she had no choice but to be pulled into his. He skipped classes, argued with professors, and eventually left school. He just had no interest in the specialized study demanded by academia.

He loved to tinker, to wander, to build. Meanwhile, she watched and observed and analyzed, and—more than anything else—followed in his wake. Somehow they made it work, and she was forever thankful for that.

Onomatopoeia

There was a screech, and then a whisper, and then near silence. The whoosh of the conditioned air coming out of the massive pipe at the edge of the dome was replaced by a hum. Everyone heard it.

And then, the ringing claxon of alarms that had never been heard before.

First Person

I didn't want Adam to go, but I knew he would. We had hours of breathable air left, and the engineers had isolated the problem as mechanical and located within the fan structure. Adam said it would be easy to fix.

I don't know why they hadn't anticipated problems. Maybe they didn't have a choice—the loss of oxygen and atmosphere came so fast. It's a wonder we're even alive and have this dome above our head.

All I know is that no one knew the physical structure and all of the complex underlying mechanical, computer, and electrical systems as well as he did. Of course they didn't. The computer guys knew nothing of the electrical systems. The electrical guys knew nothing of the physical supporting structures. They were all masters of one thing, while Adam—foolish, dreamy, insatiable Adam—knew a little bit about everything.

He told me that they called on him. No one else—him! And the pride in his voice broke my heart.

He stood in the living room of our apartment, leaned down, and kissed my forehead. He was smiling, and for the first time in our life together it didn't make me feel better. I held my right hand against my belly, and lightly grabbed his arm with my left.

"It sounds dangerous." He didn't reply but kissed me on the lips. I shook my head. "Please don't go; someone else can do this."

He took my hands in his and then kissed them. "No one else knows how everything works together like I do." He then placed my hands on my belly and covered them with his own. "Lives are depending on me."

Then he left. It wasn't until after that I realized he never denied that it was dangerous.

Present Tense

Adam crawls along the smooth metal of the fan structure. There are no access tunnels, ladders, or entryways here. Everything was assembled with the goal of just getting the air flowing as quickly as possible. The possibility that the fan itself would fail—a simple mechanical machine with few moving parts—was so disastrous a scenario that it hadn't even been contemplated. So Adam can do little more than use the suction cup anchors and hope they hold if he slips.

He painstakingly removes a panel and examines wires, connections, and plugs. He can tell it was assembled in a hurry: the welds are ragged, the wires are spliced in odd locations, and he has to use shears to cut through hastily closed and soldered access panels that the engineers hoped would never have to be opened.

He replaces the panel and moves on. He doesn't stop to think. He doesn't consider that he is approaching the blades. He focuses on finding what has stopped them from turning.

The fan looms over Adam's head. He is next to the massive casing that holds the blades, and it is only then that he realizes that he is on the rotating structure. He puts the thought out of his head and unscrews a panel directly attached to the base of the blades. He smiles and shakes his head.

A wire as thick as his thumb has come loose. It isn't even frayed or broken. All he has to do is re-attach it and tighten the screw.

It is then he realizes that once he attaches the wire, the fan will immediately begin turning. He looks down at the precipitous drop. He looks back the way he came, a slippery bridge of smooth metal that will rotate the moment he attaches the wire.

Interior Monologue

I can make it. I just have to be quick and careful. The fan will turn, but it will start slow, right? So I'll have time to get across. Violet will be waiting for me at home, and she'll be so angry but so proud, and the baby will kick like crazy, and that will make her wince and laugh all at the same time.

Of course, it is starting to turn as I tighten the screw. The flow of electricity has been restored. Okay, that makes things more difficult, but I can still make it.

Every time we pass a log, I'll show my son how I kept my balance. He'll try it and fall and then laugh and be impressed at how I did not.

Do I need to put the panel back on? No. I need to get the hell out of here. Damn, this fan moves fast, but I can do it. All I need to do is keep my balance.

Violet is waiting. Our son is waiting. They need me. So here I go. It's all about focus and control. I've never been good at that, but I'll focus now. I can't let them down.

Fragment

A slight breeze. Distant cheers. A fall.

Run-on

Adam didn't call no one called and now there is a police car escorting another car that has pulled in front of their apartment and Violet knows that something is wrong but she doesn't want to believe it but then they come in and they are talking but she can't hear more than that Adam is dead and he has saved them all and she should be proud but don't they know that she is already proud without him having to kill himself and she holds her hand against her stomach and she cries and cries and cries and then they leave and it is just her and their baby and an emptiness that she knows will never go away.

Flashback

Adam was holding her hand as they both lay on their backs on the grass, looking up at the distorted moon shining through the dome. He rolled over and leaned on his elbow. "You know, you really should find another guy."

Violet laughed. He was handsome and popular and funny and practically everything else that she dreamed about in a boy-friend. "Why do you say that?"

"Because I'll never amount to anything. You're in all the advanced programs. Everyone knows that you're in line for something special when you graduate. Hell, I can't even hold a job." He fell back onto the grass. "I'd just ride your coattails."

Violet peered at him. He looked thoughtful as he peered up into space. She punched him lightly on the arm. "You know you're a genius. I don't know anyone smarter than you."

"It doesn't matter if I am." He turned to her with a serious look on his face. "I'm a realist. I'll never be Chief Engineer or anything else important. I don't have the discipline for it, and—" He took a deep breath. "You deserve more than that."

She couldn't believe that Adam Traynor, one of the most popular guys in the entire school, didn't think he was worthy of her. It was absurd. "I don't need you to be anything more than who you are." She sat up, and he stared into her face. "You are the sweetest, handsomest, smartest, most amazing man I've ever met. That should be enough for anyone."

"I just don't want to let you down."

She leaned over and kissed him. "You couldn't."

Simile

It's like having a headache all the time, knowing that the pain will never go away and all you can hope to do is ignore it for short stretches of time. It's like someone stabbed you in the heart and then thanked you for it because it helped others. It's like someone showing you the most wonderful and amazing gift for your child, and then taking it away before your child ever receives it.

That's what it's like being married to a hero.

Past Tense

As he slipped the wedding ring on Violet's finger, Adam leaned forward and whispered in her ear, "You won't regret this."

Present Perfect Tense

She has never regretted it.

Second Person

That's right. Close your eyes, my darling. Now is the time for sleep.

Someday I'll tell you about your father, and you will be proud that you share his name. You will know how kind and generous and funny and wonderful and brave he was. And while I know that will fill you with pride and love, I know it will also hurt, because he is not here for you.

But he wanted to be, my darling; he wanted to be.

So close your eyes.

Sleep.

And breathe.

SELECTED STORIES

Mission. Suit. Self.

1. The mission is more important than your suit.
2. Your suit is more important than your life.

— Code of the Tactical Armored Infantry

A bead of sweat slid down the side of Billy's face as he surveyed the wall of green vegetation. Although the droplet of sweat didn't distract him, he was aware of it, and thus a tiny fan in his suit switched on, drying his face.

He was staking out the north, and it was a dangerous mess. The forest canopy spread out overhead, removing any satellite intel, and the ground was thick with vegetation and trees. It was enough cover to give the natives an opportunity to get close and launch an attack before Billy's squad of heavily armored soldiers wiped them out.

He considered the mission. He was running point, laying out the beacons that would mark the defensive perimeter around the planet's initial settlement. He wasn't the best in combat, but Billy saw the big picture, and the squad respected his ability to assess terrain, risk, and other strategic elements.

Billy paused and considered the native life forms. The danger from them was real. While he and most of his squad had barely paid attention during the cultural overview, they'd soaked up the tech and military briefings. The result was that while they may not have known much about what the natives looked like, they knew that the natives were extremely aggressive and had enough tech to do significant damage in the right circumstances. After the first attack, the squads didn't even bother calling them natives. They were just "hostiles."

Entering a clearing, Billy stopped and ran a full visual and auditory scan. It was more chaos: The heat and vegetation made infrared assessment practically useless, and the sound of movement was everywhere.

He did have a good view of the topography from the clearing, and while he would ideally lay a perimeter with a much larger buffer between the hostiles and the settlement, there was a valley directly to the north that worried him. With the dense trees and the steep hills to the east and west, it would be much more difficult to defend than the flat terrain he was currently standing on. The added benefit of laying the beacon at his current location was that he wouldn't have to proceed any further into hostile territory.

"Rally One, this is Niner Point. Assessing northern topography. Any secondary intel for this quad?" He spoke, and his neural connection told the suit computer which channel to use. He really didn't like the look of the valley. The whole quadrant was crawling with hostiles, and if he was going to set the northern perimeter, he wanted it to be as simple to secure as possible.

"Hold on, Corporal." There was a short pause. "Negative on that. There's a satellite village about one klick north, but that's it."

Satellite village? Fuck. Why the hell did the settlers move farther north to seed a new village before the first one was officially secure? The rest of his squad didn't have to think in those terms or consider such nuances. They focused only on the mission, and their mission was to defend the perimeter. But for Billy, things weren't that simple. He was defining the mission.

There was a distant explosion behind him, and Billy flinched. The massive armored suit suppressed the movement but identified the surge of adrenaline and activated an emergency defensive scan. Billy breathed easier as the scan revealed no neighboring activity. Something was going on to the southeast, however. His mind considered Echo Point, and the suit engaged that channel.

". . . fall back, Jackson. Ichi and J.F., advance and lay down some cover."

"Roger, Rally One. Slight damage to my left arm, but otherwise good. They're still coming, though."

He refocused on his job, and the channel went silent.

The suit had presented a map overlay of his known location and topography as he made progress. The distance to the main settlement was pretty tight if he dropped the perimeter at his current location. I should probably run the perimeter north of the satellite village, but that was definitely the more dangerous choice. As it stood, command wouldn't care either way. They just wanted a secure perimeter. Still, he decided to doublecheck.

"Rally One, this is Niner Point."

"Sorry, Niner Point. We have activity in Echo quadrant. Radio silence unless it's an emergency."

Billy looked north again. They hadn't briefed him on the village, which meant it wasn't a concern. And with the steep elevation to the northeast and northwest, no one would really question him if he decided to lay the perimeter where he stood.

Billy smiled. If the hostiles were attacking on the eastern quadrant and he laid a beacon this tight to the main settlement, his chances for getting off the planet alive were excellent. He couldn't believe his good fortune. This would be the easiest point mission he'd ever had.

He stretched his arm downward, and the suit mirrored his movement, augmented by the neural connections between the computer and his brain. A foot-long metal tube extended from the end of the arm of the suit. He couldn't feel it with his arm or hand, but he could feel the movement with his mind and nerves as naturally as if he had extended a finger. There was a click, and compressed air drove the rod into the dirt.

Continuing to the west, Billy laid two more perimeter beacons, keeping the valley to his right. With the presence of the beacons, his squad's mission was finalized: if hostiles crossed the perimeter, the soldiers in their mighty armored suits would terminate them.

———————————

He hadn't even had time to take a shower after punching out

before Cortez tracked him down.

"Man, you missed some action." Cortez lived for the moments when she was in her suit laying waste to hostiles, and she was incredibly efficient at it. Billy assumed she was talking about the attack to the east he had heard. The east perimeter was much larger, and they had two suits laying beacons.

"Don't tell me they attacked Moot. If they did, they have an uncanny sense for knowing our weaknesses." Billy smiled. He didn't get along with Moot or his squad, who he felt took unnecessary risks. Cortez kept pace as Billy continued toward the showers.

"No, you idiot. It was that village up from your beacons. The hostiles have it under siege. The civilians jumped on one of the military channels to ask for help." It was hard to frown with the amount of nerve damage from augmentation and integration surgeries, but Cortez somehow achieved it. "I can't believe we're missing out on that."

Billy slowed to a stop, taking in what Cortez had said. "I didn't pick up anything on my scans."

"They started when you were checking out. Small arms fire. Not a big deal, but dangerous for the colonists, though—they're not even in composite buildings, if you can believe that shit. Probably a bunch of Greens wanting to go native." Cortez shook her head. "They have a high-end laser defense system, but . . ." Cortez shrugged. Billy knew what the shrug meant—commercial defense systems didn't last forever and weren't foolproof. "So, why'd you bail on the village?"

Billy took a step toward Cortez. "I didn't bail on the village!"

She backed up, raising her hands. "Calm down, man. I didn't

mean it like that. Just wondering why you laid the beacons so close to the main settlement and away from the excitement. Defending a bunch of native sympathizers from the natives would have been fun."

Billy lowered his head. "It just wasn't a good idea, Cortez. A valley like that would be tough to secure."

"Well, shit, you're the guru, but we've had no problems defending worse." Cortez slapped him on the back. "But it sucks, man. Freakin' hostiles taunting us." Cortez shook her head and wandered off.

Billy knew that Cortez would probably forget the village even existed by the end of the day. Her mission was to guard the perimeter, and that didn't include the village. Everything else was a distraction. That wasn't the case for Billy. He knew that Cortez was right—they had handled tougher defensive assignments than that valley.

His mind kept flashing to the moment before he had laid the first beacon, considering whether to include the village or not. It troubled him that his main concern at the time was getting off the planet alive. Why hadn't he thought harder about the consequences of abandoning the satellite village? Billy turned away from the shower. He had to review the audio that Cortez mentioned.

Without his suit, he had to access the archive in the Comm Center. It was a long walk, an exhausting prospect on legs accustomed to augmentation. He doubted he'd see any fellow suit jockeys—they tended to avoid being in public for just that reason. The awesome image of might they projected in their suits was destroyed as they walked around on scarred, stitched-together, and often weak bodies.

There were whispers as he walked into the Comm Center. All of the personnel there had worked with armored augmented soldiers for a long time, but it was still rare to see one without his suit. A private walked him to a link, and Billy could see a look in her eyes as she shot furtive glances at him. Was it curiosity? Horror? He didn't know, and he wondered if he was losing the ability to read people's faces.

He found it right away, some unsourced audio on the channel assigned to Whiskey Point. He hit play.

UNIDENTIFIED: Hello, is there anyone there? We need immediate assistance. The Dahili are attacking from every direction, and we don't know how long our defenses can hold. Please help us. [Pause] Is anyone there? Please, there are only five of us.

LIEUTENANT FRANKLIN BOYLE: Attention: This is a military operations channel, and you are forbidden from broadcasting on this frequency.

UNIDENTIFIED: Thank God you are there. Please send help. There are five of us, and four will need medical transport. We are in the Peace Valley outpost.

[Long pause]

COLONEL GABRIEL RUIZ: This is a military channel. You need to use the distress frequency if you need help.

UNIDENTIFIED: We tried that! There was no answer.

COLONEL GABRIEL RUIZ: We are not equipped to do

search and rescue. Please refrain from using this channel.

UNIDENTIFIED: Can't anyone help? Just send a few of those men in the giant suits to carry us out? I've seen the holos of them knocking down houses with their hands. Certainly they can carry five of us to safety.

[The sound of multiple gunshots in the background]

COLONEL GABRIEL RUIZ: I'm sorry. We gave an evacuation order, which you clearly ignored. You are on your own. Now stop broadcasting on this frequency immediately.

UNIDENTIFIED: What kind of monsters are you? They have guns. You can easily stop them, but we can't! Why won't you help us?

COLONEL GABRIEL RUIZ: Whiskey Point, we are switching to backup channel two, effective immediately.

UNIDENTIFIED: Hello?

[Long pause]

UNIDENTIFIED: You bastards are just going to leave us here to die? Why?

[Unintelligible background voices]

UNIDENTIFIED: They aren't coming.

Billy sat back in the chair and took a deep breath. Everything made a terrible sense. Command had issued an evacuation order and called it a day. If someone didn't or couldn't evacuate, well, that was their problem. Still, he wished he had known all this as he was setting up the perimeter. He wasn't sure he would have made the same decision.

No. He wouldn't have made the same decision.

He punched up Ruiz. His assistant answered but put Billy right through when he identified himself. Ruiz didn't bother with a greeting. "Corporal, I don't like hearing from suits unless they're on a mission. Is there a problem?" He was gruff and sounded unhappy.

"That's why I'm calling, sir. There is a problem. I set the perimeter about one klick too far south."

There was a pause, and then Ruiz answered, "Wait, is this about the satellite village?"

"Yes, sir. It's unprotected."

"Not a problem, Corporal. There was an evacuation order." Ruiz sounded more relaxed now that he knew the topic. "You made the right decision; now go jump in the hot tub or something." The line went dead.

Five people were under assault and helpless thanks to him. He turned the comm to the channel that Whiskey Point had originally used. He tapped the talk button a few times nervously and then pressed it.

"Hello? Are you still there?" He cursed under his breath. He wanted to sound commanding but was sure he was coming across as tentative and weak. He just wasn't used to communicating outside of his suit.

He waited for someone from Comm to ask him what he was doing, but no one else was on the channel. Command must have abandoned it when the woman from the village refused to give up the frequency. After a minute or so, he tried again. His voice was more confident this time. "Hello, is there anyone there?"

— 77 —

A voice replied immediately. "Oh my God, I thought I was dreaming. Yes! We are still here." There were gunshots in the background. "Who are you? Are you coming to save us?" Her words came out in a rush. Billy didn't know how to respond. Hell, he didn't know why he even bothered contacting them. There was nothing he could do. Now all he had done was given them false hope. "Are you there?"

"Yes," Billy replied. He struggled to think of what to say, but decided to just tell the truth. "I'm sorry, but I'm not sure what I can do."

"Can't you just defend us? You have those men in armored suits. I heard that just one could defeat hundreds of regular soldiers." The voice was more confident than pleading, as if she could inspire him with her words.

"That is outside the scope of our mission." Billy said the words without emotion. Toneless. Without any conviction.

"Oh." It was such a simple word. An expression of surprise with a plaintive acceptance. She didn't object to the primacy of his mission, and her resignation made the mission seem something dark and evil, like death or a terminal illness.

"But maybe there is something I can do." Billy blurted the words out.

"Couldn't you carry us out? Maybe we could find a wagon or something and you could just come in and pull us out. Don't you do that?" Billy cursed himself. The woman had moved from acceptance to hope. Why was he torturing her with hope?

"I'm sorry. You just don't understand. We're a tactical infantry unit. Our suits don't even have hands, and the calibration needed to adjust the sensitivity of my arms would take too long." He paused trying to think of a way to explain. "I'd be just as likely to crush you as save you."

"But there's more than just you! Can't you bring more people to help? Certainly you all could protect us?" Desperation was again creeping into her voice.

Billy didn't know how to answer. They had a full squad assigned to guarding the northern perimeter and, despite his conservative assessment, he knew they could defend the village, too. But it was too late. The mission was finalized. Guard the perimeter. The village wasn't within the perimeter.

It was as simple as that.

The tactical armored infantry would fulfill their mission at all costs—it was what they did—but the moment Billy had laid the last beacon, that mission didn't include the five people in a village with no name. Billy dropped his head in his hands. He had explained the strategic reasons, but he knew the truth. He dropped the beacon south of the village because he was afraid.

The woman broke the silence. "You're not coming, are you?" The voice sounded utterly defeated. This was not acceptance. This was hope crushed under the boot of tactical armor guarding a perimeter one klick too far south.

"I'm coming." It was a quiet voice, almost a whisper, the words spoken without a hint of confidence or force.

But he had said them.

"Oh my God, thank you!" Billy didn't answer. He didn't have any idea what he would do, and he didn't know what to say.

After a period of silence, the woman spoke again, her voice a whisper. "So what's your name?"

"Corporal Billy Whitaker." He tried to sound confident, to sound like the savior he had just promised, but he couldn't.

"You're going to get in trouble for this, aren't you, Billy?"

He thought of his training, the words "mission, suit, self" repeated again and again until it was part of his psyche. And here he was abandoning the mission and putting both his suit and himself in danger.

"Yes," Billy finally said. The woman didn't reply immediately.

"My name is Ruth. The other four people here are Tom, Ahmed, Iona, and Julie. We are all nice people." She paused. "That's worth getting into a little trouble, isn't it?"

"Yes." The answer sounded small and inconsequential, and Billy wasn't even sure he said it loudly enough to be heard. But he meant it, and the fact that he did frightened him, because he had no idea what he would do. "I need to go, Ruth." It sounded strange saying her name. She was now a person. Not a mission, a person.

"Thank you, Billy. Thank you so much."

Billy walked as quickly as he could to the staging area. He worried about how long their defenses would hold up. He guessed they had a motion-activated defense system in place. It probably had a battery strong enough for a limited number of strikes, but the hostiles wouldn't know that. That was the good news. The bad news was that they were clearly testing it every so often, and the commercial batteries weren't meant to handle constant laser fire for very long. Billy picked up his pace.

No one gave him a second look as he lowered himself into his suit. Between the long hours on duty, the neural connection to the computer, and their own bodies augmented to work with the suit and not outside it, most soldiers preferred to spend as much time suited up as possible, sometimes even sleeping in their suits. He punched in the ordnance for ground combat. That also wouldn't generate attention: it wasn't uncommon for off-duty soldiers to be pulled into ongoing missions. Five active-duty suits were already assigned to the northern perimeter, but Billy wouldn't have been surprised if there were more than ten out in the field.

Claws dropped from the ceiling and detached his arms. His physical arms went numb as the neural connection to the suit's nerve center stopped having anything to connect them to. His arms glided down a track and disappeared into a storage area. The claws returned with larger arms, the hands made of cannon barrels and the forearms embedded with specialty munitions—rockets, flame throwers, and chemical weapons. The arms were placed in position and, after several twists, the claws retracted. The suit reconnected his nerves, and Billy felt his arms tingle.

The suit's arms now attached to him could hardly be considered arms at all—fingers replaced by cannons, forearms embedded with lasers, shoulders mounted with defensive countermeasures—but they felt entirely natural to Billy. They were his arms. He ran his final systems check and then took a deep breath.

Billy Whitaker, the strategic pride of Phoenix Platoon, had no idea what he was going to do.

He set off with the simple idea of just fighting his way to the village and then holding off the hostiles for as long as he could.

It was a ridiculous plan. He would destroy countless hostiles, but eventually one of them would get in a lucky shot or he would collapse in exhaustion.

He couldn't see any other result. He would be beyond the perimeter and, in the culture of mission-suit-self, he would no longer be part of the mission. No one would come save him. As he half-heartedly returned the wave of the technician on duty, Billy realized an even more depressing scenario: Command might just destruct his suit by remote before he even had a chance to get to the village. Still he continued onward.

His earlier route to the perimeter was now wide and clear, the thick vegetation and small trees crushed under the feet of the numerous, massive suits that had marched past. Fallen tree limbs lay strewn along the path, and laser burns scorched the trees that were still standing. Billy checked his HUD constantly even though he didn't need to. The valley to the north was as clear as the perimeter line marked by the beacons he had laid earlier.

He knew that once he hit the perimeter line, the path would split to the west and east, where the thump thump thump of armored suit legs walking the path would be an auditory warning to the hostiles, while the pounded dirt they left behind served as a visual one. Beyond the crushed earth of the perimeter line there would be nothing but thick vegetation and trees.

They had five suits guarding the northern perimeter, and Billy assumed that he'd have a decent chance of meeting one of the guys from his squad at some point, but when he reached the intersection he was alone. He attempted an infrared scan, but it was once again useless. He went silent and did an enhanced audio scan.

He could hear an approaching suit from the east, its telltale footsteps obvious. There was rustling all over the forest in front of him, but he couldn't make out any voices. He heard sporadic gunfire from the north, which filled Billy with relief. The village's defenses were still holding.

Taking a deep breath, Billy stepped across the perimeter.

Less than ten seconds later, a concerned voice filled his head. "Billy, is there a problem? We have you advancing. Have the hostiles engaged?" Billy turned off all of his comm channels. It suddenly struck him that if command didn't know what he was up to, they wouldn't destruct his suit. He heard one of the suits pounding toward him, so he plunged ahead.

After about fifty meters—and without thinking—Billy stopped for a standard initial mission assessment. As he realized what he was doing, Billy shook his head. How could he assess a mission that didn't exist? He ploughed on.

He skipped the full visual-range scan and kept to human-visual. There was some movement at one o'clock. Audio picked up voices. Then there were voices at ten o'clock. He heard the click of native weaponry being armed. He cursed and charged straight north.

The gunfire started a few steps further and came from every direction. His earlier briefing told him to expect a high volume of hand-held projectile fire, which was low-risk against the heavily armored suits. Billy ignored the constant barrage of bullets and rushed forward.

The vegetation blocked much of his visual range, and he was moving so fast that he ran right into several groups of natives. They were bipedal with reptilian skin and large eyes that protruded from their heads. Their four arms allowed them to carry multiple weapons, creating the high volume of fire Billy faced. He ran right past them.

He burst past a tree and hit the last thing he had expected to see. The hostiles had created their own perimeter: a pathetic patchwork of tree trunks piled in a loose wall from east to west, hidden from the recon satellites by the dense foliage above. There were more gaps than wall and it was little better than tissue paper against a suit, but what it did provide was confidence, and that worried Billy more than anything. Bullets were hitting him from every direction.

He knelt slightly and spread his arms. He felt his skin open and the weapons extend as the suit launched missile grenades at the barrier to the left and right.

Pieces of bodies and wood flew amid bright explosions. Despite the carnage, the rate of fire didn't decrease at all. The bullets continued to bounce off his faceplate, chest, and limbs. He retracted the missile launchers into his arms, strode forward, and extended the cannons that acted as his hands. High-caliber bullets shredded the barrier in front of him.

Screams filled the air, and Billy adjusted his aural range to focus on the low and very high ranges. He didn't want to hear screams. He wanted to hear wood snapping, footsteps, and guns firing. He leapt the ten meters over the remaining barricade. There was a high-pitched sound from behind, and Billy switched to his rear view and initiated defensive countermeasures.

The lasers mounted at his shoulders turned and filled the

woods with a lattice of deadly light. Shredded leaves fell like rain. Tree limbs fell. Anything that moved was pierced and sliced by the lasers. Three hostiles near a concealed cannon fell to the ground in pieces.

But it was too late.

The first and only shot from the cannon hit him below his right shoulder, knocking him forward and to the ground.

Billy jumped to his feet and recalibrated, maxing out three-hundred-sixty-degree countermeasures while he did field assessment. Both lasers were still functioning and were firing at anything that moved.

Bio came out normal, but the right arm of his suit dropped to twenty percent functionality. It was a disaster. He hadn't even gone a hundred meters, and his suit was badly damaged. He closed his eyes, disengaged audio, and thought, the lasers flickering in the background his only distraction.

What he really needed was his squad. You could encircle a squad, but you couldn't surprise one with a cannon shot in the back. Drops of sweat started to form on Billy's forehead, and the suit engaged its fans.

He tried to put thoughts of the squad behind—they weren't going to save him or the village. They would observe the perimeter. That was their mission, and if anything defined the power of the corps, it was their rabid devotion to finishing each and every mission, no matter how small—even if it meant leaving suit, civilian, or friend behind.

And in the depths of that cold knowledge, a solution formed in Billy's head.

He turned back toward the perimeter and re-oriented the systems for maximum defense and speed. The cannons in his arms retracted, and the lasers on his shoulders switched to full power.

He leapt back over the demolished barrier and turned to the southeast. An alarm started to sound: the battery was exceeding its safe operational range. He silenced it. There wasn't much else he could do. He needed full power for his defensive lasers and full power for traveling at speed.

The hostiles hadn't anticipated him rushing back south, and the ones who now operated the cannon fled in disarray as he attacked them. The lasers took out the hostiles while he crushed the cannon itself with two blows from his left arm. He rushed onward, running parallel to the northern perimeter.

And there it was: the first beacon. At this point, Billy was more concerned with Command than the hostiles. He didn't know how they would react if they realized what he was doing,.

He knelt down, gunfire striking him in the back but, with the lasers wreaking destruction within close range, the rate of projectiles had significantly slowed. He reached for the beacon. With his combat array, all he had was a small, two-pronged maintenance claw. The rest of his suit was nothing but weapons. He reached for the beacon but it slipped. God, please make this work. He wiggled the beacon and then pulled again.

It slid out.

He held the beacon against this chest with his damaged right arm and ran. He could hear another suit approaching from behind and to his left. Wondering if they would try to stop him, he arrived at the second beacon. It came out easily, and he ran to the last one.

Cortez was standing next to it, motionless in her suit.

Billy ignored her and knelt down and worked on the beacon. There were some explosions, and he looked up. Cortez was wreaking destruction on hostiles in every direction. Her missile launchers were firing in harmony with her cannons in a terrible symphony of destruction. Missiles shattered trees, cannons flattened logs, and screams bled into the upper range of Billy's audio.

Billy stood up and opened up his external speaker.

"The perimeter is moving north, Cortez." She nodded, her faceplate mirroring sunlight and falling leaves. She didn't move.

Billy felt the heat of the battery against his skin so he turned off the lasers and put all energy into field assessment and mobility. He sprinted toward the valley. With the beacons cradled against his suit by his right arm, he had to avoid even small trees rather than just knocking them out of his way. He had every sense turned to the max. The sound of gunfire and ricochets off his suit were constant, but he tuned them out.

Focusing on sound, Billy avoided areas with heavy hostile audio indicators. It took him longer but he side-stepped immediate danger. After a few hundred meters, the gunfire slowed down. He switched to full visual and could see the lasers from the village firing in the distance. He passed the village, added a fifty-meter buffer, then knelt down. The rods tumbled out of his right arm. He grabbed one with his working claw and shoved it into the dirt. He awkwardly pounded it in with the barrel of a cannon. He fumbled with the other two beacons, cradled them under his arm, and moved east.

He had just laid the second beacon when his audio warnings

screamed. It was too late. A cannon shell smashed into his back and threw him forward in a rolling mass of metal. He slammed against a tree.

He tried to engage his suit's countermeasures but found them to be nonfunctional. He did an emergency assessment. The suit had cushioned his body so he remained unscathed, but the suit itself was ruined. Arms nonfunctioning. Legs nonfunctioning. Helmet mobile but visual nonfunctioning. All other functions failing.

Billy ignored them all.

The new perimeter was incomplete, and he had to set the final beacon. Billy initiated his emergency disengage protocol. The wires that connected his brain to his suit retracted into the box at the base of his skull. He suddenly felt deaf and blind.

Plugs that connected the nerves up and down his arms, legs, back, and body jerked out as his suit opened. The smell of forest decay, burning ozone, and dirt staggered him as he collapsed to the ground.

Billy Whitaker, half naked, nerves raw and senses over-whelmed, looked around. He heard rustling somewhere in the trees as his eyes alighted on the last beacon, lying on the ground five meters away. He half-ran, half-stumbled to the beacon, picked it up, and ran east.

He surprised a hostile, who didn't fire as Billy ran past him. Of course, they are expecting a suit. That thought was short-lived, however, as a bullet whizzed past his head. The shot must have alerted the hostiles, for he could hear them rustling through the vegetation in every direction.

As he considered whether he had gone far enough, Billy felt

a bullet smash into his left arm. He cried out and reflexively tried to turn on maximum defensive countermeasures but then remembered—he wasn't in his suit. Leaves rustled and branches cracked. It's now or never, Billy.

He stopped, pressed the edge of the beacon into the ground, and leaned all his weight against it. It had slid about six inches when another bullet hit him in the leg. He fell to the ground next to the beacon, pulling it downward with his body. Another bullet hit him in the side of the chest.

Looking up, all Billy could see was green, a beautiful verdant green. In the distance, he heard an approaching thump thump thump, and then he started to cry. He had lost his suit. He had lost his self. But the mission lived on.

SELECTED STORIES

The Sky Smells Blue Above the Clouds

Rosie escaped to her backyard, the private place where the fence hid everything but the sky overhead. She liked the pristine lawn, the majesty of the single oak tree in the corner, and her dad's Adirondack chair, the wood cracked and warped but still comfortable. But more than anything she loved the smell of the grass.

The grass was freshly cut, and Rosie lay down on it. She closed her eyes and ran her fingers through the blades, focusing on the cool, almost wet, sensation on her skin. Touch was nice. Touch was uncomplicated. Like grass. Rosie turned her head, and the shorn edges of the grass caressed her cheek as she took a deep breath. The smell filled her vision. It was green. Grass smelled green. Simple blessed green.

She didn't mind that it was a pale green, like the Crayola color Magic Mint, product number 58 in the large box of 120 crayons that Rosie memorized in school when she was trying to explain her synesthesia to her teachers in a way they could understand. They did, but her classmates didn't. No—correction—they understood, but they didn't understand.

Her favorite smell was the perfume Ms. Lindy wore every Friday: number 11—Blizzard Blue. It led her to imagine that Ms. Lindy would throw snowballs or build snowmen after school on Friday, even at the end of the school year when it was too warm for long sleeves, let alone snowmen.

And while Magic Mint the smell of grass wasn't the same as Green the look of grass (number 45, or sometimes Forest Green--number 38, or Fern--number 37), it was still green. She tried to explain to her friends how wonderful it was for smells to look like they were supposed to, but they just laughed. When she said that it was rare and comforting, they just laughed harder.

Most colors smelled different than they looked, but there were many where the dissonance was so sharp and unexpected that it was painful. Roses, which looked beautiful in the fullness of their red (Scarlet, number 100) smelled like the sickly orange of Neon Carrot (number 70). And oranges--oranges were just confusing. How could an orange not smell Orange (number 72)? But no, oranges smelled like Cornflower (number 30).

The worst, however, was the floor cleaner they used at school, which made everything smell like Atomic Tangerine (number 6). She had been yelled at countless times for running down the hall as she tried to escape the awful pervasive color. As her friends hung out near their lockers, they would get mad and call her a jerk or loser as Rosie excused herself and left the halls as quickly as possible. Rosie couldn't stand being in a place where everything and everyone was tinged with the puke orange of Atomic Tangerine.

She squeezed the grass in a fist as she remembered trying to tell all the others how hard it was to see two colors for the same thing. Oranges weren't Orange, they were Orange and Cornflower; Roses weren't Red, they were Scarlet and Neon Carrot. Countless other things didn't look how they smelled. Why could no one understand how painful it was to have your vision betrayed by your smell?

There was only refuge: Black. Rosie would keep her eyes closed in class, at restaurants, even walking. She ran into things. Her classmates constantly tripped her or spit on her or did things she couldn't feel or see, only hear. Eventually she didn't know what was worse, the pain of Black (number 10) or the pain of her brain fighting over two colors.

Rosie opened her eyes and looked at the sky. Crayola really got the sky right. The blue wasn't Denim (number 33), it was Sky Blue (number 108), and the fluffy white clouds were White (number 126). She gave Crayola a pass on the sun because you're not supposed to look at the sun, and besides it's so bright could you know what color it really was? Of course it helped that she couldn't smell the sky.

And what did it smell like up there? Did anyone really know? What did it smell like above the clouds? If she were to float up and away from all the ugliness that filled her life as she tried to reconcile conflicting sights and smells would she find a different world, a world where things actually smelled like how they looked?

She imagined what it would be like if her miserable mixed up life suddenly made sense in the heavens. The moon would smell Gray (number 44) or even the oddly named Manatee (number 61). Mars would smell Red (number 94)--definitely not Scarlet, as roses looked Scarlet, and she didn't need to remind herself that roses that looked Scarlet smelled Neon Carrot. This was her world, after all. Venus? Not Green or Yellow or any boring variation of those but Mountain Meadow (number 67). Why not? Make the others make sense of her life for once.

Finally, she would look down from the heavens and smell Earth. It would be wondrous, magical, welcoming. All the painful things would be too small to see, too distant to smell. Gone. Nothing would smell of Julie's Razzmatazz (number 93) shampoo as she shoved Rosie's face in the toilet asking her what color shit smelled like or Carol's Unmellow Yellow (number 120) body spray as she tripped Rosie in front of school for the millionth time. An orange wouldn't smell like Cornflower. Atomic Tangerine wouldn't exist. From the heavens the Earth would look and smell the way Rosie always wanted: A majestic flawless panorama of Turquoise Blue. Calm Turquoise Blue.

Number 119.

Biographical Fragments of the Life of Julian Prince

JOHN JOSEPH ADAMS
ON "BIOGRAPHICAL FRAGMENTS OF THE LIFE OF JULIAN PRINCE"

This is my favorite story that I've published in Lightspeed. I just love the inventive way in which it tells the story via excerpts of Wikipedia entries and news articles and interviews, and how it forces you to construct this meta-narrative in your head as you read it. It is only 5,000 words and yet feels so much bigger.

Julian Prince

From Wikipedia, the free encyclopedia

Julian Samuel Prince (March 18, 1989 – August 20, 2057) was an American novelist, essayist, journalist, and political activist. His best works are widely considered to be the post-Impact novels *The Grey Sunset* (2027) and *Rhythms of Decline* (2029), both of which won the Pulitzer Prize. He was awarded the Nobel Prize for Literature in 2031.

Prince was a pioneer of Impact Nihilism, a genre that embraced themes of helplessness and inevitable death in the aftermath of the Meyer Impact. His travelogue, *Journey Into Hopelessness* (2026) outlined Prince's return to North America, ostensibly to survey the damage to his home state of Texas. The book's bleak and powerful language of loss and devastation influenced musicians, artists, and writers worldwide, giving voice to the genre as a counter to the rising wave of New Optimism, which sprang out of the European Union as a response to the Meyer Impact and the enormous loss of life. [1] [2]

Early Life

Not much is known of Prince's early life. He spoke rarely of his childhood, and with the loss of life and destruction of records during the Meyer Impact, little source material remains. What is known is that Prince was an only child, the son of Margaret Prince (maiden name unknown) and Samuel Prince. He was born in Lawton, Oklahoma, but moved to Dallas, Texas, when he was eight years old.[3] In an interview before his death, Prince noted:

> I was a good kid, a boring kid. I didn't cause trouble, and trouble didn't find me. I studied hard and planned on being a journalist, figuring that I was better at observing the world than shaping it. I graduated high school, and continued with my journalism classes via the net. Up until the Impact, I was thoroughly and utterly average.[4]

Upon earning a bachelor's degree from Khan University in journalism, Prince embarked on a career as a web reporter.[5]

Excerpt from Julian Prince's Nobel Prize Acceptance Speech, 2031

So it is that life, to which we all cling with desperation and joy, prevails. Yet I cannot let go of the memories, the experiences, and the physical reality of those that have passed away. The ghosts are all around us, even as we squint to see through them. It has been said that I deny optimism and ignore our future, but that is not true. It is just that I refuse to let the difficult questions remain unasked. I refuse to conveniently ignore the graveyard that is now half our planet. And I refuse to feel joy that so many have lived when so many—so many—have died.

It is with humility that I accept this award, not for myself, but for the hundreds of millions who are not here with us today. I did my best to tell their story, but they deserve so much more than I can possibly give. If I achieved even a small part in doing so, I am glad.

Pre-Impact Career

Prince spent the decade before the Meyer Impact crossing the globe courtesy of a series of freelance journalism jobs. His first writing job was with AOL Local/Patch in 2010, where he aggregated citizen journalism stories from North Texas and rewrote them for syndicated release to the net. He continued to work for AOL Local for seven years, until he quit in 2017.[6] He wrote about this transition in an essay on the carefree lives of the pre-Impact world in 2031:

> I quit because I wasn't excited. Can you imagine such a thing today? To leave security and stability because your life just isn't dangerous or crazy or exciting enough? Such was the innocence before the Impact. So I left the boring to move to Africa, where the excitement was, and where I could write about

things that shed light on life and death,
not ennui or entertainment.[7]

Prince took a job with European news agency Star News in 2017. His writing up until the Impact in 2023 was spare and fact-driven, although flashes of Prince's eye for emotion could occasionally be seen. Prince would say of those years, "Everything I wrote back then was worthless, but it was also worth everything—because it was the mind-numbing limitation of facts and cold description that allowed me to view the Impact in its true light." [8] [9]

Excerpt from "Maldives' Last Grain of Sand," reported by Julian Prince (Star News, 2018)

Ahmed Manik sits in a rickety wooden boat, watching as a wave crests over a strip of sand. Manik is the grandson of Maldives' last President, Mohammed Manik, and the strip of sand is all that's left of the island country of Maldives, a country wiped away by global warming, rising water levels, and decades of mismanagement. Scientists don't even bother estimating how long this last remnant of the former island nation will remain before it is washed away. It may be weeks, perhaps even days.

Manik shrugs when asked about the lost legacy of his family and former country. "We are all grains of sand, just waiting to be washed away," he says and smiles, which accentuates the heavy creases around his eyes and mouth. He may have accepted the inevitable force of the rising waters, but it has taken a toll.

Impact Year

Prince was already in Africa during the six-month preparation for the Impact and thus didn't have to take part in the Expatriation Lottery. He wrote many news articles during this time, but no fiction or essays. There is no record of Prince's life for the 18 months following the Impact and the immediate global environmental catastrophe it caused. Prince would write about this time often, but never about his own life—only what he had seen.[citation needed]

Excerpt from "Immigration Concerns Dominate South African Presidential Debate," reported by Julian Prince (Star News, 2023)

Cheers followed South African presidential candidate Maxwell Mahlangu on each stop of his tour of the country, despite deep concerns that his endorsement of the United Nations Emergency Emigration Plan for North America would upset the entire framework of the country. "Our country's motto is 'Unity in Diversity,'" Mahlangu said at a rally in Port Elizabeth. "How can we let these people die simply because we refuse to accept more diversity?"

Later in his speech, Mahlangu touched upon a common theme expressed by leaders across the globe as countries prepared to take in refugees from North America—no one really knows what the Meyer Asteroid will do to the world. With a massive death toll a certainty, the real economic unit of the future may be people, so taking in immigrants is a good idea: "No one knows what God has in store for us and what life will be like. In the future, with more people, South Africa will be stronger!"

Sitting president Jacob Sisulu rejected Mahlangu's moral and economic argument. He continued to object to the UN's current plan for South Africa to accept up to a million expatriates from the United States. "Such a wave of people would severely stress every part of our country," Sisulu explained during a press conference in Pretoria. "They will starve! China or Russia or Europe should take them!"

"Coming Home"

In 2025, Prince's essay "Coming Home" was published in Der Spiegel.[10] It became a worldwide sensation and ironically helped create the New Optimism movement that Prince's later work would reject. In the essay, Prince described the unloading of thousands of North American refugees in various cities along the African Coast, using the metaphor of humanity leaving its doomed colonial past to come home to Africa.

Literary critic Gerald King described the essay as the perfect origin point for both Impact Nihilism and New Optimism, and its publication immediately marked Prince as the leading light of post-Impact literature:

> The central concept of "Coming Home" is warm and welcoming. Africa, the cradle of civilization, is welcoming home its wayward sons and daughters, even after their many sins. The deep themes of forgiveness and generosity fed directly into the New Optimism being loudly voiced in Europe. But many overlook that Prince did not flinch in describing the gaunt, guilty looks of those that exited the boats—a few million survivors while hundreds of millions of their friends and family members were doomed to die back home. The language that Prince uses in describing those left behind is very stark and makes it clear to the close reader that one should mourn, as well as celebrate. [11]

The reception of "Coming Home" led directly to Prince tackling the difficult subjects of the Impact and "the Lost," a term for those who died in the Impact that Prince coined himself in *Journey Into Hopelessness*. [citation needed]

Excerpt from "Coming Home" by Julian Prince (Der Spiegel, 2025)

Not one person who landed in Africa looked over his or her shoulder. It was as if the direction labeled "West" no longer existed. Sunsets were no longer a thing of beauty but a painful reminder of those doomed across the ocean, a literal dying light. Thoughts stopped at the ocean. It was overwhelming to consider friends and family alive yet suffering with the knowledge of their impending deaths.

Denial was the coping mechanism of choice. No one that landed in Africa could remember having any family or friends remaining in North America. I asked dozens of refugees, and none would admit to having left anyone behind. Friends, neighbors, colleagues, family—they all somehow made it into the expatriation program.

In Mogadishu I met a man I used to work with. I asked him about several of our former colleagues and whether he knew if they had been chosen to expatriate. He denied ever having known them. I was shocked for a moment, but recovered and asked about his family. He smiled and said that they all made it and were settling across various cities in Europe. He didn't know anyone that had been left behind.

No one knew of anyone left behind.

To know was to be a participant in their death sentence, and that was too painful, too sad, too horrific. But the guilt existed, nonetheless. So they did what they could to avoid it. They didn't look West. They didn't watch sunsets. They never called or messaged North America, even as it still lived. They cut off their former lives and looked ahead to their new ones.

And thankfully, mercifully, Africa was there with open arms. A return to home and hearth, as it had for time immemorial, made everything better.

"The Conscience of a Generation"

Prince traveled back to North America to survey the damage from the impact in early 2026. He spent six months traveling across the continent with a United Nations Blue Team, observing and sometimes helping as they assessed the damage. This experience was the basis for his worldwide best-selling travelogue, Journey Into Hopelessness. His stark and often graphic descriptions of a barren landscape, littered with dead flora and fauna, were described by critics as "poetic," "beautiful," "poignant," and "chilling." Prince himself described the trip as the "hardest six months of my life. It was like performing an autopsy on your own parent."[12][13][14]

After returning from North America, Prince spent the next six months working on his first piece of fiction, the novel The Grey Sunset. The novel follows the life of Phil Gumm, who is a working class truck driver from Kansas and a winner of the Expatriation Lottery. The novel is highly introspective, and the narrative follows Gumm's descent from exhilaration at being one of the lucky few to the depths of guilt over those he left behind. The bulk of the novel takes place on the journey from Galveston, Texas to Capetown, South Africa, and the physical journey is an extended metaphor for the emotional and spiritual journey that Gumm also takes. As Gumm physically gets closer to safety and a new life in Africa, he emotionally and spiritually gets closer to guilt, despair, and, eventually, suicide.[15]

The book was released at the height of the New Optimism movement and was immediately heralded as a compelling counter. The phrase Impact Nihilism had already been in use since the publication of Journey Into Hopelessness and similar works, but it was *The Grey Sunset* that defined the genre and helped propel its popularity.[citation needed] *The Grey Sunset* won the Pulitzer Prize in 2027, which had been re-established by the Expatriation Heritage Foundation the year before.[16]

Prince shied from publicity, and spent the bulk of the next two years working on what many consider his masterpiece, Rhythms of Decline. The novel is a complicated narrative of five families, each of whom lives on a different continent. The centerpiece is the impending impact of the Meyer Asteroid, and how each family deals with an uncertain future. Only one family survives the Impact, although their future is full of doubt as the novel ends.

Literary critic Malcolm Spencer described the book as "the

work of unparalleled genius." He described the American Smith family, as "the definitive representation of our times. They face impending death with a kind of sad and yet warm acceptance. They live one day at a time, knowing that days are all they have left." Spencer described Prince as "the conscience of a generation" for his unflinching look at the tragedy of the Impact and the guilt and pain it left behind.[17]

Some critics saw the book as a complete repudiation of New Optimism, and this led to significant criticism of Prince. London web daily The Beacon called Prince "The Prince of Doom and Gloom."[18] The Paris Review printed a scathing review of *Rhythms of Decline*, describing it as "one man's self-absorbed journal of guilt over surviving the Impact."[19]

Prince did a series of interviews in the wake of the criticism. His most famous appearance was on the popular holo The New Day, broadcast out of Berlin. When asked about his critics, his reply became one of the most quoted lines of the post-Impact era: "I'll listen to them when they've walked among the three hundred million ghosts that I have."[20]

Despite the controversy, *Rhythms of Decline* won the Pulitzer Prize and led directly to Prince being awarded the Nobel Prize for Literature two years later.[21]

Excerpt from Journey Into Hopelessness by Julian Prince (Vintage/Anchor, 2026)

Finally we landed in Texas.

When I was young my parents took me to Palo Duro Canyon in northwest Texas. It was a massive rift in the Earth that my mother told me God himself had carved out of the Texas plains. I didn't see it that way. I saw it as a broken land born of violence, something left behind when the plains and hills had collided. But broken as it was, I saw it as natural and beautiful. The sharp angles and the bare rock acted as a balance to the plains that spread into the distance. And despite the wound in the land, life continued to thrive around it.

There is nothing natural or beautiful in the tortured land that now covers North Texas. The force of the impact stripped away everything. There are no trees, no plants, no grass. There is nothing but scarred land, windburnt ridges, and fetid water. Everywhere there is decay, death, and the certainty that this is a barren land with no future.

———————————

Excerpt from an interview on The New Tonight Show (Canal+, January 18, 2030)

Phil Preston: Speaking of your trip, there are rumors that you didn't get along with the UN team during your visit to North America.

Julian Prince: Well, we spent six months together, so there were the normal conflicts, but I wouldn't say that I didn't get along with the team. I actually have a funny story about it.

Preston: You have a funny story? This I've got to hear.

Prince: Since this was officially a military mission for some idiotic reason, the scientists and I—all the civilians—had to take part in an orientation. The orientation was basically our team leader, Colonel Cooper, telling us over and over again that he was in charge and we had to listen to him. He was this husky bald guy with a kind of soft voice, but he had an intensity that made it clear he was used to people doing what he told them to do. His look and demeanor reminded me of Marlon Brando's character of Kurtz from the movie Apocalypse Now, so when he finished I said something like, "Sure thing, Kurtz."

[Audience laughter]

Prince: I thought it was funny, too, but he didn't seem to get it, and he marched over to me, put his nose right up to mine, and said, "The name is Cooper, and you can call me Colonel or Colonel Cooper." Of course I called him Kurtz for the entire six months.

[Audience cheers and laughter]

Preston: I'm surprised he didn't do anything.

Prince: I just assumed that he had no idea who Kurtz was, but during the last few days of the mission I said to him "I'm going to miss you, Kurtz." No one else was around, so I hoped he realized that I meant it. He then shook his head and said—and I remember every word to this day—"You have been calling me Kurtz this entire trip, and I had hoped by now that you would have realized how foolish that has been." He then leaned in and whispered in my ear,

"You can't go native when there are no natives."

Preston: Wow. That's intense.

Prince: I know. And people call me the Prince of Doom and Gloom!

[Scattered audience laughter]

Preston: Actually, do you mind that—when people call you the Prince of Doom and Gloom?

Prince: [Pause] Yes.

Preston: Well, you've dated Janet Skillings, so I'm guessing that being the Prince of Doom and Gloom hasn't interfered much with your love life.

[Audience laughter]

Prince: Well, being rich and famous helps.

[Audience laughter]

Preston: So is there anyone in your life right now?

Prince: I'm afraid not. I live life one day at a time.

Preston: So what you're saying is you're only up for one-night stands.

[Audience laughter]

Prince: Life is a one-night stand.

[Uncomfortable silence]

Political Activism

The next ten years of Prince's life were marked by political activism. Violence in Africa and Asia led to the rise of the

Repatriation Movement, which fought for the return of former North Americans to their home continent. While most countered the movement on practical grounds—North America simply wasn't habitable yet—Prince saw the movement as something deeper and darker. He felt the movement was about rejecting Africa and Asia and the expatriates' hosts more than a desire to return to their devastated homeland.[22]

In a widely quoted speech in 2034, Prince said:

> This is not a movement about returning home. This is a movement about rejecting friends. This is not a movement about finding comfort in familiar lands. This is a movement about fearing those who wish to help. This is not about repatriation. This is about rejection.[23]

Prince was a prolific essay writer during this period, but nothing ever approached the popularity and power of his earlier work. His essay "Rejecting Home" (Der Spiegel, 2035) an acerbic and politically pointed update of his essay "Coming Home," was described by critic Gerald King as "a sad attempt by Prince to leverage his earlier brilliance to make a point about what many are starting to see in him as a naïve perception of unity in people who want no such thing."[24]

Prince ceased his anti-repatriation activism when parts of North America were re-opened for settlements in 2038.[citation needed]

Excerpt from *Rhythms of Decline* **by Julian Prince (Knopf, 2029)**

Simon had hoped that all would be normal in the end. He would tuck Annie into bed, pat Arthur on the head, and then kiss them both goodnight. Jason would wander off, falling asleep to the dull glow of some video game or another. Later, Simon would poke his head in, mutter a goodnight, and then turn the electronics off. Finally, he and Annie would hold each other and let the night take them. That was his dream—that they would fall asleep as a family and never wake up.

Yet, somehow, this seemed better. Their tears, their grief, and their fear tapped into a well deeper than family ritual. They were together in a moment when being alone seemed profane and wrong.

Jason joined Simon and began to cry as they all held each other. No one said anything. They breathed the air that gave them life. They shared the love that made them family. They cried the tears that made them human.

And then they died.

Later Life and Novels

Prince lived the rest of his life in Capetown, South Africa. He only published three more novels; all were well-received but garnered far less praise than The Grey Sunset and Rhythms of Decline. [citation needed]

Countdown (Knopf, 2040) told the story of a young man named Franklin Proudman who had decided to repatriate to North America. Proudman lands and finds life a lot different than he expected. Much of the book is a rambling series of anecdotes around the hopeless efforts of Proudman to build a life. He eventually dies from starvation, the ground still too damaged to produce crops.

Lost in North America (Knopf, 2045) is Prince's only foray into the science fiction genre.[25] The novel tells the story of the Winkler family, who hide in a fallout shelter in Rapid City, South Dakota. Despite Rapid City being ground zero for the Meyer Impact, the family survives and exit the shelter a year later to rebuild their lives. When it becomes clear that there is no food or wildlife, the family begins a journey, foraging for food across North America. The book has clear allusions to Cormac McCarthy's The Road, but the emptiness of the landscape provides for a uniquely Princean view. The book generated significant positive critical press.[26][27]

Prince's final novel, Crater (Knopf, 2056), was released the year before his death. The book continued his exploration of the dark aspects of repatriation.[28] The novel follows a scientist, William Ho, and his assistant Wendy Singh, as they attempt to descend to the bottom of the Meyer Crater. Like Prince's other novels, *Crater* is rife with introspection. As Ho and his assistant get closer to the bottom, they realize they are in love. It is when they have reached ground zero of the Meyer Impact when the two realize they have found their future together. The novel's ending is ambiguous, as the two are attempting to climb out of the crater but are uncertain if they will ever escape. While thematically similar to his earlier novels, *Crater* employs a denser prose style, with long paragraphs that often include a stream-of-consciousness technique. Despite its ambiguity and often dark scenes, the novel was marked by some as a return to the optimism of "Coming Home." *Crater* was a bestseller and re-established Prince as a popular figure in post-Impact literature.[29][30]

Personal Life

Prince was romantically connected to several celebrities during his life, including actresses Renee Diaz[citation needed] and Janet Skillings.[31] None of these relationships lasted more than a few weeks, however. In 2050, unofficial Prince biographer Susan Nillson announced that she had uncovered proof that Prince had left a girlfriend and child behind in North America. The document, a digitized copy of a Texas State birth certificate backed up on a European server, showed that Prince fathered a child named Samuel to a mother named Wendy Reynolds. Prince never acknowledged Nillson's allegations, although most contemporary historians consider the claim accurate.[32]

Excerpt from Julian Prince's final interview (Paris Live!, 2056)

Aliette Rameau: You've achieved so much, Monsieur Prince. Do you have any regrets?

[Pause]

Rameau: Monsieur Prince?

Julian Prince: I'm sorry. Your question is a bit overwhelming. My life is full of regrets.

Rameau: Is there anything specific you could share with us?

Prince: No. [Takes drink of water] I'm sorry. Could we change the subject, please?

Death and Legacy

Prince died on August 20, 2057 in Capetown, South Africa, from a self-inflicted gunshot wound. He left no suicide note. Having died without any heirs, Prince bequeathed his literary estate and assets to The 300 Million Ghosts Foundation, which was founded to record, research, and archive the stories of those who died during the Meyer Impact.[33][34]

Prince's legacy continues to define and influence artists to this day. While Impact Nihilism has fallen out of fashion, Prince's stark images and deep themes can be seen in everything from the paintings of Ellen Winslow to the music of the Bluefins. His use of introspection and stream-of-consciousness has influenced writers as diverse as Joe Lguyen and Isabel Shoeford.[citation needed]

The play *Coming Home* debuted on the anniversary of Prince's death in 2058 at the Globe Theater in London. Adapted by Nobel-winning playwright Andrew Hillsborough, the play was an unabashedly optimistic look at a world that survived an extinction event and came away smiling. Hillsborough noted on BBC, "Oh, I'm sure old Prince would have hated it. But the words are all his. Somewhere along the way he changed. Just because he decided that facing the abyss meant that we were all doomed to fall in, doesn't mean we have to agree with him."[35]

Epitaph on Julian Prince's gravestone

"Finally home."

SELECTED STORIES

Looking For Bad Guys

Carter's mom pinned the cape around his shoulders, brushed out the folds, and then stood back. Carter glanced in the mirror and nodded. A superhero looked back at him. Spinning around, Carter loved how his cape billowed behind him. His mom clapped her hands. "That's my hero!" Carter stopped, said goodbye, and then marched out the front door. It was time to patrol the neighborhood.

The first person he saw was Big J. Big J sold stuff from his Dodge Charger on the corner of Henderson and Flatts. He was a cool guy who often gave Carter money for hanging around and letting him know if the police were nearby. Carter always got the feeling that Big J already knew when the cops were there, but he would smile and give Carter money anyway.

"Whoa, C-note. What's that all about?" He called Carter C-note, although he hadn't ever given Carter more than five dollars.

Carter turned just enough to give his cape some lift and then thrust his arm in the air and made a fist. "I'm fighting bad guys!"

"Sweet! You want to go check on your sister then. She was arguing with Rip. Might be some trouble there." Big J winked.

"I'm a superhero. I don't get involved in arguments."

Big J shook his head and then replied, "Well, superhero, I have a job for you then. Why don't you go find her and send her my way. I got a delivery up at the college, and if she's arguing with Rip, she ain't doin' any more tricks for him tonight."

"I'm fighting bad guys." Carter repeated, putting his hands on his hips and letting the words speak for themselves.

"Sure, C-note. I get it. But you could patrol the neighborhood on the way there."

This made sense to Carter, so he spun around, his cape marking his departure with a flourish, and made his way up to Rip's place. Along the way he didn't see any bad guys, just the Langdon brothers, who were throwing rocks at the third story windows of the abandoned school. They were getting angry because they couldn't reach them, and all the windows on the first two stories were boarded up.

Rip had a storefront on Kensington, and Carter admired the way his office had real leather furniture and how clean it always was. Rip even had Lionel, who was like seven feet tall and three hundred pounds, guarding the door. Rip was a real businessman. Carter's mom was always badmouthing Rip and arguing with Kelly over him, but Kelly made a lot of money so her job must have been pretty good.

He walked in and Lionel immediately commented, "Rip, we got us a superhero!" Carter held up his hand, and Lionel gave him a high five, which was more like a low five for him. The girls sitting in the chairs didn't say anything.

Carter looked at Rip. "Carter, if you're here to cry about Kelly, you can leave right now."

Carter put his hands on his hips. "I'm just delivering a message to her and then--" He paused for effect. "--I'm fighting bad guys!"

Rip stared at Carter for a moment and then laughed. "Of course you are! Well, she went home." He paused and then added, "But I can give you some info on where to find bad guys."

"You can?" Carter figured this was true since he had a bodyguard.

"Sure, but it's secret. Come here." Rip nodded toward the girls, put his finger to his lips, and then beckoned him with a wave.

Carter nodded his best solemn superhero nod and walked over behind Rip's desk. "I'm listening."

Rip leaned down and whispered in Carter's ear, "This neighborhood is full of bad guys. Sick evil motherfuckers." Carter's eyes went wide. "But here's the thing—they're hidden. They may even be right in front of you." He then leaned back and talked in a normal voice. "You don't need to look for bad guys. You just need to recognize them?" He laughed and shook his head, but Carter ignored him as he considered the words.

It made so much sense. Bad guys were always hiding. He was foolish to think he'd find them out in the open in alleys or on the street. They may even have had alter egos or disguises. He'd have to check out everyone.

An hour later he trudged into his house. "What's wrong, baby?" His mom was sitting in the living room watching TV with

Kelly, whose lip was cut and swollen.

"I can't find any bad guys."

His mom stood up and rushed over. "Hush now. You have plenty of time to be discoverin' bad guys. No need to be growin' up too fast." She unclipped his cape. "Next time use your imagination, baby. That's why God gave it to you."

Carter nodded without enthusiasm. He could use his imagination, but he wanted to fight real bad guys.

Maybe someday he'd find them.

Perspective

BRIAN WHITE
ON "PERSPECTIVE"

This is one of the first stories I bought for Fireside, and it has stuck with me over the years. A young man, trying to make his mark on a broken city and a broken father. A mark that can't be washed away, but that no one can really see, or understand. It's an evocative story, full of washed-out color and decay and just a little light, the spark of a son's mission. I'm glad it crossed my path.

The worst part about picking my son up from the police station was the walk to get there. I hadn't been outside in years, but it was still the same—the drab gray of the smog-stained overcast sky, the decaying concrete, the stench of gasoline, urine, and who knew what else. But thanks to Jeffrey there was a new assault to my senses—black molecular paint permanently defacing an already wretched city.

With every step I could see his work—his "tags" as the police called them. They were all different, and there was no rhyme or reason as to what he would vandalize—the sides of buildings, street surfaces, retailer kiosks, even windows. The randomness made catching my son a difficult task for the police, but catch him they did, and now I had to walk these vile streets to bring him home.

I paid the bail, followed the directions to processing, and waited for my son. The policewoman there was polite and offered me a seat, but I stood. I wasn't in the mood to relax, and Jeffrey needed to see how angry I was. So I waited, arms behind my back, staring at the door that led inside.

His head hung low as he walked out. He glanced up at me and then lowered his head again. "Hi, Pop," he mumbled. I didn't move. He walked over and added in a whisper, "I'm really sorry."

"You lied to me." I grabbed his right hand and pulled it up between us. "These black stains aren't paint, Jeffrey. That is your skin. It was the price to pay for your job, you said. I'm painting ships with a new kind of paint, you said. You made the stains sound like a worthy sacrifice." I tossed his hand down.

"Pop, please. Let's talk about this at home." He looked around the room, shifting from one foot to the other.

"Yes, we will discuss this at home." I turned and walked out the door. He followed. I walked the streets again, Jeffrey shuffling behind me. I focused on the concrete at my feet, unable to bear looking at his work. My hands were clenched tight enough to turn my knuckles white, so I shoved them in my pockets.

I closed the door and set all the locks. I couldn't remember the last time I had left the apartment for the drab world outside, and I did not intend to do it again. Jeffrey followed me in as I sat in my media chair and stood near the door. The distance felt greater than the span of a room. At least he was quiet and respectful. I sighed.

"The lies are what bother me the most, Jeffrey."

He stiffened. "I never lied."

I frowned and raised my voice. "You never lied? You said you were working at the shipyards!"

"I did work there. I painted ships."

"Did you, now? Or were you defacing them in the middle of the night?" I pounded my hand on the arm of the chair. "I was sad, but I was still proud of you, Jeffrey. All those art lessons. All those awards. That you couldn't make a living with your art broke me up inside. But to see you finally turn your art into industry, even if it required your hands to be stained that horrible coal black, that was a price I could at least understand. You were doing something meaningful."

As I shook my head, he interjected, "I am doing something

meaningful, Pop." His voice rose. "You just don't understand!"

"Painting permanent black marks across the city is not meaningful. This 'tagging' that the police told me about. It's a mark of pride, they said. A way for gangs and others to know that this is your city." I closed my eyes and lowered my head. "I thought I had raised you better."

"Pop, I wish I could explain, but I'm not done. When I am, you will understand." He looked so earnest and so sad. I stared at him, and he lowered his head. Despite his hope, I knew I would never understand. How could I? He was marching off to scar the city again, and he expected me to just accept it. I couldn't.

I stood up. "Not done? You have shamed me, Jeffrey. Made me leave my home. Lied to me. And you are not done?" I walked over and waved a finger in his face. I considered striking him. I had never done so, and perhaps that was my mistake. Perhaps I was weak, raising him alone and not wanting to bring him any more sadness and pain than he had already experienced through the death of his mother.

A tear slid down his cheek, and I lowered my hand. "You don't understand, Pop." He said it in a whisper, then turned and strode down the hall to his room. I sat back down and dropped my head into my hand. I wasn't sure where I went wrong.

Other than a few curt questions and answers, we didn't talk during breakfast the next morning. Jeffrey seemed distracted and troubled, and I didn't want to intrude. I felt that he had finally come to his senses and was working up the courage to apologize to me and present some kind of plan for turning his life around. So I gave him his space.

I was shocked, then, when he grabbed his keys and walked toward the front door. "Where are you going?" I asked, none too gently.

"I have work to do, Pop. Please let me be."

I hurried over to him and grabbed his arm. "You are not leaving this apartment." I held tight. "What work could you possibly have to do? Tagging some neighborhood dogs? Maybe getting arrested again, so I have to leave my home and walk these cursed streets?"

He pulled his arm free and turned to face me. "That's the problem, Pop. You never leave the apartment. Ever since mom was hit by the car, all you've done is sit in your chair and look at old photos and read old books." He was animated, and his desperate tone didn't anger me so much as make me sad. "I've begged you to come with me, somewhere, anywhere. Hell, Pop, you won't even go on the balcony."

I dropped my arm back down to my side. I wanted to ask what this had to do with his delinquency. I wanted to ask why he was attacking me when he was the criminal, but he looked so concerned for me that I felt I had to respond. "There is nothing outside for me. You've seen how the city has changed. There is no beauty left. It's all gray and drab. Why would I voluntarily walk through such a depressing world? Why would you want that?"

He shook his head. "I get it, Pop—clouds, concrete, smog. You've said the same things for years, but there is beauty in the city." He walked to the door, opened it, and then turned back to me. "Mom saw it." He closed the door behind him. I stood for a long while, unmoving, staring at the door. At some point I went to bed.

———————————

A day later I had unlocked the front door and considered going out to look for him, but I never opened it. It would have been hopeless searching amongst that sprawling compost heap.

I phoned the police on the second day and asked for help, but they already knew that Jeffrey was wandering the city. They called me back the next day. There was no bail this time.

I asked what happened, and the policeman curtly told me to just check the news. I did. Jeffrey had painted non-stop since he left our apartment in a manic attempt to spread his tags across the city. The judge who originally allowed him bail was being pilloried by the press for releasing the infamous "Nanotagger" the first time. It wouldn't happen again.

I hadn't watched or read the news, so I didn't realize that Jeffrey had generated worldwide attention. To some he was the new Banksy. To others he was a new breed of criminal, permanently vandalizing the city. To me, he was my son, my misguided, damaged, motherless son.

I ignored Jeffrey's calls. His messages were plaintive requests for me to come talk to him, but I just couldn't do it. What was there left to discuss? His final message was a request for me to attend his sentencing. He had something important to say, and this would be his last opportunity to say it to me in person. I was sure he assumed

I wouldn't leave the apartment to visit him in prison, and he was probably right. So when he asked if I would come as one last show of fatherly love before he was gone, I knew I would.

I made the walk to the Laura Tejeda Memorial Courthouse. It was the big one halfway across town, which made the walk only worse. Even the bright windows of the glass buildings did little more than reflect concrete and smog. High up one building I noticed the black paint of Jeffrey's hand. It was little more than an oval. I tried to see it as art, but could not. It was just graffiti. Ugly black graffiti.

The press was everywhere. Microphones were thrust in my face, holo-cameras with bright lights aimed at me. I ignored the shouts of "Mr. Chapman!" or the rudely personal "Bill- Bill Chapman!" and shoved the microphones aside. People stared at me as I walked down the courtroom aisle, but I paid them no mind and sat near my son. He saw me and smiled. He wiped his eyes with a thumb and forefinger and then looked at me again. He held up his forefinger, as if telling me to wait.

It didn't take long. Jeffrey pled guilty and that was that. The judge asked if Jeffrey had anything to say. He stood up. His hands were shaking as he turned and faced the people packed in the courtroom. "I want to apologize to the citizens, officials, and merchants of the city." His voice trembled and was almost a whisper. I doubt many heard him. But I did. "I cannot explain why I did what I did, but I do accept responsibility for my actions."

Jeffrey then turned to me and started crying. "Pop, I have so much I want to say to you about what I did, but I'm afraid you won't listen. So, I'll just ask you for a favor, one simple favor." I lowered my head. I didn't know what he wanted, but I was sure I couldn't help him. The thought of being powerless to help him brought tears to my own eyes. "Pop, all I ask is that you go out to the balcony of our apartment, look around the city, and think of me." He wiped his eyes with his sleeve. "It may not be a lot, but it would mean a lot to me."

He then turned to the judge and stood quietly as he was sentenced to ten years in prison for maliciously defacing public and private property. The fact he used molecular paint was ultimately the real problem. He stole it from the shipyard, and stealing nanotechnology—even paint—was a felony.

I walked home, and the city was even more depressing, if that was possible. I sat down in my chair and pulled out the computer. I spent the rest of the afternoon looking at baby photos of Jeffrey playing with his mother. I cried.

I went to bed without stepping onto the balcony. I knew what Jeffrey was trying to do. I knew that he thought I was agoraphobic and that having me at least step on the balcony would be a step to freeing me from our—my—apartment. But Jeffrey just didn't understand. I walked to the police station. I walked to the big courthouse. I could leave whenever I wanted. I just didn't want to. The city and world were just too ugly.

The next morning I checked the news. It was the same story. Jeffrey was an anti-establishment hero. Jeffrey was a symbol of the cancer eating away at the city. I closed the computer window. The last thing I saw was a holo-image of Jeffrey standing in the courtroom.

I looked through the dining room. The curtains to the balcony were closed. I may have failed him as a father, but I could at least do this one last thing for him. It was silly and stupid, but it meant something to my son, so I did it. I walked over, opened the curtains, and looked out into a sky of gray clouds and smog. I shook my head and opened the glass sliding door.

I walked outside and over to the railing. I looked down at the city my son had used as his canvas. The view staggered me, and I grabbed the railing for support. I looked across concrete sidewalks, streets, glass, buildings, and kiosks—all of them permanently marked with black brush strokes. Each mark was a small part of a majestic, gorgeous whole—a painting of my wife as big as the city itself.

I held out my hand into the air, reaching through the distance to touch a piece of art that was untouchable. My wife's eyes, the curve of her cheek, even the mischief in her smile. It was all there.

I couldn't believe the scale of Jeffrey's accomplishment. Each small piece of black paint was part of a whole that could only be perceived from this balcony, this exact spot. She looked back at me—the city, my wife. She was beautiful.

Ten years was too long to wait to hug your son, but sometimes you don't have a choice. I wiped my eyes and moved my chair out to the balcony.

SELECTED STORIES

A Memorial to the Patriots

A Memorial to the Patriots
A project by Andreas Villencz

Help fund A Memorial to the Patriots, a marble monument in Baton Rouge to the valiant and brave defenders of Houston, who lost their lives to the terrorist insurgency forces last year.

Official Note

This project has been approved by the Domestic Security Agency as not being a wartime risk. Participants have been pre-approved for a waiver to publicly discuss war-related topics, but only as necessary to further this project.

About the Project

The images of the terrorist attacks on Houston still haunt us: The policeman holding the dying child, the buildings in rubble, the famous video of Colonel Davis--"the Hero of Houston"--pulling and leading countless children to safety while he ignored his own injuries, and the dead birds and squirrels that lined the roads after the water supply was poisoned. There were so many tragedies that day.

But there were also many heroes. This project is about honoring the heroes.

The funds will go toward procuring the land and materials, paying the artist, and installing a monument to the defenders of Houston. The monument will be located in downtown Baton Rouge. There are similar monuments in other cities, and the participants feel that it is their patriotic and moral duty to honor these men and women in similar fashion in Baton Rouge. Further stretch goals will help fund monuments in other cities.

About the Project Coordinator

Andreas Villencz was in Houston while the horrific attacks took place. The experiences forever changed him, and while continuing his education in Political Science at Loyola University he was filled with the desire of thanking those that helped save others. Villencz approached long-time friend and artist Chris Handel with the idea of a string of memorials across the country, and the project was born.

About the Project Consultant

Josef Harte was a professor of Political Science at Rice University during the terrorist attacks. He subsequently moved to Loyola University, where he was hired as the newly created Professor of Contemporary History. He is a worldwide expert on the Houston Attacks.

About the Artist

Chris Handel gained attention after winning the National Patriotic Art Competition for her piece, "Houston." The piece is a large six foot by six foot abstract expressionist rendering of the pain of the patriots who suffered that day. She painted it with her own blood. It currently hangs in the Capital Rotunda. While she is best known for her painting, she was trained at the University of Houston as a sculptor, and she will bring her keen view of tragedy as seen in "Houston" to the marble she has chosen as her medium for the memorial.

About the Rewards

Level One
An autographed print of Handel's "Houston." Note: We have been given a waiver, and the print does not count against wartime paper rations.

Level Two
Your name inscribed as a backer on a plaque near the monument.

Level Three

An all-expenses paid trip to the unveiling ceremony. (The DSA has guaranteed an expedited interstate travel approval process for a backer from outside of Louisiana).

Risks and Challenges

This project has been pre-approved by the Domestic Security Agency, so the standard risk of the National Security Board canceling the project post-funding is NEGLIGIBLE.

Other risks include:

An inability to procure the land for the memorial after the funds are raised. The Project Coordinator is in discussion with the government of Baton Rouge, and we are confident that this risk is SMALL.

The inability of Handel to complete the piece. We consider this risk SMALL, and have plans to approach alternate artists if this does take place.

Unforeseen circumstances. During wartime there is always the possibility of disruption or challenges. We consider this risk MODERATE but also have multiple contingency plans in place for various scenarios.

UPDATE ONE

We want to profusely thank the Domestic Security Agency for their support of this project. That we haven't seen any terrorist or insurgent attacks since Houston is a testament to the aggressive steps they have taken to ensure our safety. The next time you see a DSA drone, remember to salute! It's the same sentiment we're trying to embrace for this project--honoring those that died protecting us. We open for pledges tomorrow, and I could not be prouder of what this project is all about.

--Andreas

Comment: So proud. God bless you. – Joe Bradshaw

Comment: Couldn't afford Level One but will pledge some money anyway. Thank you from Baton Rouge. – I.M.

Comment: I've waited so long to say this publicly: I lost my wife and sister-in-law at Houston. They were in the American General Center blast. They deserve to be remembered for the heroes they were. Thank you so much for this, and thank you DSA for the discussion waiver. In war it is frustrating that so many positive voices can't be heard due to the danger from the extremists. I will pledge at Level One, but you deserve more. – Tony

Comment: Folks, although we have a wartime waiver, let's keep the comments on the project. The DSA are big supporters of this, but we don't want to cross any lines. - Andreas

UPDATE TWO

AMAZING!! THANK YOU! THANK YOU! THANK YOU!

We are almost half funded after one day. We can do this! Think of the patriots! We will honor our heroes! I'll have another update on Monday. Let's be 100% funded by then!

--Andreas

Comment: Not sure if you know this, but there was an article about your project in the local paper. – J.F. in Baton Rouge

Comment: We can make this happen. - Frances

Comment: [Redacted by Domestic security agency]

Comment: You have some gall "Concerned" posting a comment like that. "Freedom fighters" don't poison reservoirs or kill children. You sound like just another weak and spoiled brat that doesn't have the maturity to deal with things that are needed for YOUR safety.

I didn't lose my leg in Houston dragging bleeding children from a collapsing building just to hear unthankful asses like you whining about things you can't hope to understand and sympathizing with the terrorists who caused that suffering. You make me sick.

You want privacy? You want to avoid long lines on your vacation drives to the Grand Canyon? Well, let me tell you what your choice is: You can have those things, but you'll have them when you are dead. Because those are the types of things that will lead to the violence that will kill you and your loved ones.

I've seen it firsthand.

The good news is that the terrorists are routed. They can't even organize or communicate thanks to those things that "Concerned" mentions. So we should all be thankful. All of us.

I am pledging to this not because I'm one of those honored but because of people like "Concerned" above who need reminded of what their ignorance leads to. – Col. James Davis, retired

Comment: Oh my gosh, the Hero of Houston posted! I am so honored that you are taking part and am incredibly thankful for your sacrifice, Colonel Davis. And a reminder to others: The DSA will delete comments that are not related to this project, exceptions like Colonel Davis notwithstanding. - Andreas

UPDATE THREE

I am stunned. I don't know what to say. My thoughts and prayers go out to the people of Baton Rouge. My God
--Andreas

COMMENTS CLOSED

UPDATE FOUR

God bless the residents of Baton Rouge.

We obviously will need to change our project. We considered canceling it, but Josef, Chris, and I felt that this would not honor either those that died in Houston or those that died in Baton Rouge. We want to honor our heroes, and we refuse to let the terrorists destroy such a noble and important goal. Otherwise they win.

We have talked this over with our representative of the DSA, and we have tentative approval to continue. Yes--our project is looked on that positively by them. However, there will be a few changes to the project:

Comments are closed. Frankly, we were lucky to get the first waiver, but with the attack on Baton Rouge, any discussion of wartime items—including memorials—is just too dangerous.

The Level Three Reward Level has been rescinded due to the new travel restrictions put in place. It has been replaced by Chris Handel offering a unique art piece for the person pledging. This is an amazing reward, and we are incredibly thankful to Chris for this. The deadline has been pushed back three weeks for obvious reasons.

And the biggest change, and the one that breaks my heart: We obviously cannot place our memorial to Houston in Baton Rouge, so we have decided to host the memorial in Shreveport. This is a much larger city, and our original funding levels would not cover the cost of procuring central property for the memorial, but—and here is the good news—the city of Shreveport has donated part of their downtown park for the memorial!

The only stipulation is that we expand the work to include the patriots of Baton Rouge, which we will happily do. So this project lives, and it is now a memorial to the patriots and heroes of Houston and Baton Rouge.

So thank you everyone. Thank you, DSA. Thank you city of Shreveport, and thank you supporters. We WILL honor them!!!

--Andreas

UPDATE FIVE

Just a short update as we've been very busy, but I'm glad to announce that we are almost fully funded! So tell your friends!

--Andreas

UPDATE SIX

I know the project was listed as suspended for the past two weeks, but it is now back. I am not allowed to say more than that we were "under review" by the DSA after the chemical attack on Shreveport. And for those who used to live or know people who lived in Shreveport, my thoughts and prayers are with you.

After such a horrible Spring, it appears that things are finally returning to normal. For those who are uncertain, let me repeat what I was told by someone that I cannot identify: "Please continue. You're doing good work. Don't let an awful coincidence ruin what is a patriotic initiative." He also repeated what we all know from the news--the extremists have been smashed and are retreating, and we should be confident about moving forward.

With this in mind, I'll have an exciting update in two days.
--Andreas

UPDATE SEVEN

We are delaying things while we wait for approval for something exciting. Please be patient!
--Andreas

UPDATE EIGHT

I'm so sorry that this has taken so long, but I have good news: We have decided to place the memorial to honor our heroes in Dallas!

In addition, we will expand the monument to all the heroes and patriots who have lost their lives during this insurgency. Thanks to our consultant Josef who assessed that the biggest and safest spot in the entire Southwest was also the logical new location for our monument. We had to wait a long time before we could get approval, but as we've seen every step of the way, the DSA really does support our patriots and wants to see this project move forward.

I feel compelled to update our risks with the following notes:

The risk of unforeseen circumstances is now NEGLIGIBLE due to our new safer location.

The risk of procuring a location has increased to MODERATE due to building restrictions, public access limitations, and the nature of the large urban center we have chosen. This risk is offset by the support of our project by the DSA and our patriotic supporters.

I hope you agree that these risks are small for such an important monument. I'll provide an update in two weeks.

--Andreas

NOTICE!

You have accessed a site that has been identified with known terrorist connections.

Your access ID and IP address have been logged.

If you have any information about the persons connected to this site or project ("Fund a Memorial to the Patriots") contact your local Domestic security Agency office. Those who live near the remains of Dallas, Texas, should contact one of the temporary field offices established in Ft. Worth or Austin.

Click the link below for additional information.

Closure

I clench the bag of peanuts with my right hand, thinking how my dad will respond to the gesture. It's a pathetic gift, and I'm tempted to just leave it on the floor of the elevator. Ted takes my left hand and squeezes it. He looks at me as the elevator door closes. "You okay?"

"Just tired," I reply. He nods. He thinks I'm talking about dealing with my dad, and I am--but it's Ted, too. He wants a happy family that cannot exist, and I'm just not strong enough to tell him. He shuffles his feet but doesn't say anything.

We're up to the third floor, and I'm thankful for the quiet when he adds, "You're going to tell him, right?" It's a whisper. I nod my head, but he's no longer looking at me.

"I told you I would." He squeezes my hand again. I feel a frustration I am all too familiar with. When only one answer is acceptable, why bother asking the question?

The elevator dings, and I let go of his hand as the door opens. We walk past the nurse station to the waiting room. The nurses know me by now and make momentary eye contact, their smiles as antiseptic as the smell that permeates the entire building.

I enter the waiting room, all plastic ferns and pastel prints. My mom and sister are there. Mom notices me and stands up. "David!" She walks over and hugs me. She lets go and then holds my arms in her hands and looks me in the eyes. "Are you sure you have to go?"

I sigh. I get all the questions without the happy answers. "I'm sorry, mom, but I told you I just can't afford to stay. I've used all my vacation days and a whole week of unpaid vacation."

She clenches her teeth but doesn't say anything. I know she's disappointed, perhaps even angry. The thing is I can't blame her. Just like I can't blame Ted. They just want things to be happy. Hell, they just want things to be normal.

I look over her shoulder at my sister. "Hi, Jean. Who's with Pop?"

Her legs and arms are crossed. She has always hated the silence and the tension demanded by Ted's and my visits, and this visit has lasted so long I can tell she's fed up. She nods toward the direction of Pop's room. "He knows you're leaving today and kicked everyone out until you got here." That's my dad, all right.

Mom squeezes my arms. "He wants to be alone with you before you leave." She stares into my eyes. She looks concerned, but I can't tell if it's for me, my dad, or both of us. She lets go of my arm and holds up a finger. "You know how he is, so don't be angry with him. He loves you and is just disappointed you won't be here for..." She can't say it, so she turns to Ted. "Are you okay, dear?"

"I'm fine, Ruth." He pats me on the shoulder. "Just trying to be there for Dave."

"You're a wonderful friend." There is no irony in my mom's voice, but I catch Jean rolling her eyes.

"Is Pop awake?" I cut in. "We have less than an hour."

"Oh, yes. He was just waiting for you." I turn toward the door with Ted following when my mom says, "I'm sorry, Ted, Arthur only wants to speak with David." There is no malice in her voice, only pain. "It may be their last father-son time." I am relieved. I can handle the clarity of my dad's venom better than Ted's or Mom's conflicted neediness.

"Of course. I'm so sorry. Of course," Ted stammers, and there is real hurt in his voice, but it is not for himself. He is sad that he somehow put himself before someone else. I stare at him as he turns away, and in that moment I love him so deeply I want to share it with everyone, including my dad.

He walks over and sits down next to Jean. "I'll just wait here with you guys." Jean takes his hand. She always liked Ted, but the gesture is so intimate, so familial, that I almost can't move. Is this what it's like in a normal family?

As I consider the question, my mom kisses me, and I realize that I need to go see my father. I glance at Ted, say I'll be back in a bit, and leave the room.

I knock on my father's door and walk in. I had been there the day before, but that was with the rest of the family. Then there had been conversation, hushed laughter, and calm denial. Now there's no hiding from the fact that he looks drawn and sickly. His skin is yellowish, and the tubes and wires--so easy to ignore amidst movement and talk--stand out as a stark exclamation that my father is dying.

"Hi, Pop." I walk over to him and put my hand on his arm. He looks at me but doesn't say anything. His arms rest on the blanket like desiccated tree limbs on fresh snow. His neck doesn't look strong enough to support his head. But his eyes--his eyes are very much alive.

I let go of his arm and sit down. I place the brown paper bag on the table next to the chair and cross my legs.

I wait, and he finally talks. "I'm sorry my dying is messing up your schedule."

"Jesus, Pop."

"Hey--" He holds up his hand, palm out. "It's fine. I'm used to not being a priority."

I try to be calm and not sound frustrated. "Pop, you know the moment that they said you were terminal I flew out here. I've used all my sick days, all my vacation days, and a week of unpaid vacation. I can't just sit here and wait without any income." As soon as I say the words I feel miserable.

Pop frowns. "I'm sorry I haven't died fast enough for you."

"That's not what I meant, and you know it. The doctors said you had days to live, and I rushed here to be with you. I was scared." His face doesn't change. "I'm happy that you are still with us. I want you here. I don't want to see you gone."

He turns his head away from me. "But you are leaving, and I'll be gone." I nod even though he can't see me. Perhaps because he can't see me. I couldn't much deny it--this was the last time we'd ever see each other. He turns to me, and I can't tell if he's angry or sad. "So how long do we have?"

I pause. He is asking about my flight, but the question could just as easily refer to his mortality. It's probably not unlike the question he asked his doctor two months earlier. Finally, I reply, "A little less than an hour, give or take."

He smiles. "So, how do you want to spend your last hour with your dad?"

"Don't be like that, Pop."

"Heh, when the doctor tells you that you don't have long to live, you get used to accepting final moments." He is smiling, and I feel a little better. My father has always been tough and strong, and I prefer that dad, laughing in the face of death, to the angry and bitter dad I'd known for the past few years.

"You that close?" I say it but immediately worry that I ruined the moment. The words were too blunt, too cruel.

My dad laughs. "They've told me the same thing for weeks now. 'We can't say exactly, but it won't be long.' 'Your cancer is very advanced.' So what the hell do I know?" He coughs, and the smile disappears from his face. I realize that speaking more than a few sentences at a time strains him.

I wait until his breathing settles and then ask, "How do you feel?"

He shrugs, but winces afterwards. "I piss in a tube. I'm on so much dope that it's not even fun anymore. The nurse is a bitch and ugly, too. I sleep all the time but always feel tired. My family keeps me company by playing shitty board games and letting me win." He squints at me. "I hate when people let me win." He doesn't laugh, but he doesn't cough either. He swallows hard.

"That doesn't answer my question." I press the point, not to be cruel but because I really need to know. Maybe it's fruitless, but

I have hope.

"It won't be long, Davy. Not long at all." He turns his head away and coughs. I reach for his water but as I touch the glass to his hand, he waves me off. His coughing fit over, he wipes his mouth and eyes with a washcloth and looks back at me.

He hadn't called me Davy in a very long time.

I'm sorry I lost the game, dad.

You didn't lose the game, Davy. It's baseball. It takes a team to lose a game.

I dropped the ball.

The pitcher let the batter hit it. It's a team game. Nothing worth crying over.

I'm sorry, dad.

Listen, there will never be anything that you'll need to be sorry about with me. Did you do your best?

I tried.

Think about the game. The whole game. Did you make the right decisions during the game, even if you may have failed in the process?

I think so.

Then that's all that matters. Try hard. Do the right thing. That's all that matters to me.

Before I say anything, he says, "So why'd you come?" His arms once again lay still on his blanket. His voice is raspy and weak, but the words have force, and his eyes--they continue to pierce me.

"How can you ask that, Pop? You're dying. Of course I'm going to come see you. My God, what kind of son do you think I am?"

"I don't know. You tell me."

I don't reply, and my dad shakes his head. I can tell my silence disappoints him, but I don't know what to say. "Can't answer the question, can you? Well, let me answer for you. Rather than college you leave for New York. You have some kind of job helping feminists and socialists get their message out. You come home once every few years just to shake hands and kiss babies whose names you don't even know."

He pauses even though I know he's not done speaking. I wait. "And--" He stops, and it would be so easy to cut him off as he struggles for words. I could change the subject, lessen the tension. But I don't, even though I know what he wants to say. Maybe I need to know whether he will actually say it. "I can't believe you became a homosexual." He waves a hand. "The other stuff I could live with. But that?" The question hangs in the air.

You promise?

Yes.

It's just not healthy keeping our relationship from your parents. What's the worst that can happen?

Well, he's dying, Ted. What do you think is the worst that could happen?

That's not funny.

I'm sorry. Look, we're leaving tomorrow. I'll tell him. He's dying, and we shouldn't have any secrets between us.

Exactly. Why don't you tell him today? That way we could all spend some time together as a family. I mean, you tell me constantly that he was a great dad until you left for New York. I'd like to know that dad.

I don't think that's a good idea.

Fine.

Don't be like that. I'll tell him tomorrow. If I tell him today and he takes it poorly then everyone will be miserable. I mean, I'm sure mom knows but if my dad freaks out... You know.

I don't know.

Just trust me, will you?

I do. Just promise me you'll tell him. It's important.

I promise.

I look at his intense eyes, and I see expectation, sadness, hope, and fear in them. He had never mentioned it before, and now, in his final moments, he has. I feel defeated. I get all the unhappy questions, and I'm tired of the unhappy answers.

"Where the hell did you get that idea? I'm not gay!" I throw up my arms. "And you told me you always wanted me to be independent. 'To be my own man.' So I go off to New York, work my ass off to make a living from the ground floor, and every time I come home you're disappointed I didn't stick around." I pause and look at him. I can't read his face. "I just didn't know what you wanted, Pop. Did you want me to improve myself like you always told me to do or did you want me to stick around and weld iron at the shipyards?"

I put my hands in my lap. They are shaking. I had never spoken back to my dad like that in my life. I almost expect him to pull a belt out from under his hospital bed and use it on me.

"You're not gay?"

The expectation in his voice makes the words come easy. "Is

that it? All those judgmental looks. All those complaints about New York. All those angry tirades about wasting my life. Those were all about you thinking that I'm gay?"

"If you're not gay, who is Ted? You guys do everything together. He's spent weeks here with you." He squinted his eyes. "I'm not stupid, you know."

"He's my friend, Pop. He wanted to support me, and he had a ton of vacation time saved up. I told him about the beach, the college girls, and it's Spring. He loved the idea of a vacation with a ton of hot girls here that would fall all over a guy from New York. You think he'd pass that up?" I paused and then smiled. "If you weren't in the hospital, you'd see. He's had a different girl in his hotel room each night for the past three weeks."

He doesn't look convinced. "You've never introduced me to a girlfriend."

I lean forward. "Pop, I can't say this in front of mom, but what if I told you that I don't want or need a girlfriend." I lean back. "This is so awkward." I pause for effect. "I've not been exactly been looking for Ms. Right. I've been kind of working my way through a number of Ms. Right Nows."

For the first time in as long as I could remember my dad has a huge smile on his face. He points at me with his finger, and his arm motion isn't weak or shaky. It is sure and firm. All he says is, "New York," and shakes his head.

I shrug and laugh. "The city that never sleeps."

"I can't believe you didn't tell me this. I wasn't always married, you know!"

"Pop!"

He chuckles. "Look, let me give you some fatherly advice." He pauses and tries to look stern, but the corners of his mouth can't stop from turning up in a slight smile. "First of all, I'm glad you didn't tell your mom this." He points his finger at himself and then at me and then back to himself. "This is our little secret." I nod. "Secondly, I'm sure it's all fun and exciting now, but you need to start settling down. You can't just live your life alone. Ted's only going to stick around until he knocks some girl up or finally realizes you don't have tits." He laughs hard enough that he starts to cough. I reach for his water, but he shakes his hand at me again.

"You need a woman who cares about you." He speaks each word between a cough. When he finishes coughing, he adds, "With big tits!" And after his second breast joke, he laughs so hard that he falls into a violent coughing fit. It's bad enough that it shakes his whole body. I stand up and help him sit up. I hand him his water, and he takes it this time. He stops coughing and looks weak and drawn, frail. But his eyes still are bright, and he is smiling.

"Why didn't you tell me?" It's a raw whisper, his throat strained from his coughing.

"Because that's creepy, Pop," and we laugh together. It scares me how easy the happy answers come, how amusing they are.

"Son," it's barely a whisper. I look closer, and my dad is barely there. His eyes are closed, and his hands are still.

"I'm here, Pop."

"What's in the bag?"

I had forgotten about the gift I brought. "They're peanuts, Pop. You always loved peanuts when you took us up to Orioles games."

There's a smile, but his eyes don't open. "I'm not allowed to eat anything like that, but I'm glad you brought them. Why don't you give them to Ted? Maybe he'll call it even after you disrupted his life for three weeks."

"Well, he got laid a lot, Pop."

He suppresses a laugh as he holds his hand against his chest. "There is that."

I enter the waiting room, and my sister, mom, and partner all stand at once. Mom speaks first. "How did it go?"

"It was fine. He's asleep now. Everything's fine." I look at Ted and nod.

Before anyone can say anything else, I hug my mom.

"We have to go, mom."

She is still for a moment and then kisses me on the cheek. "Will you be back for the funeral?"

I can't believe the courage it takes for her to ask such a question. I hug her tight. "Of course."

I hug Jean goodbye, and we leave.

In the elevator, Ted turns and blurts out, "What did he say?"

"He said he knew all along." The answer comes easy, and I smile at the joy on Ted's face.

"I knew it! People aren't stupid, Dave." He pulls me into a hug. "So he wasn't disappointed?"

I shake my head as we part. "Actually, he was most interested in talking about us both settling down. In fact, he asked me to give you these." I hand him the bag of peanuts.

Ted's eyes are glistening. "Oh, man. That's so awesome!" I

smile while Ted continues. "You are an idiot. How many times did you say to me that telling your dad would break the family apart?" I shrug. "At least you told him before he d--" He stops and lowers his head. "I'm sorry." I grab his shoulder and squeeze. There is nothing to say.

The elevator dings, and the door opens. As we exit Ted adds, "Your dad is a cool guy."

The Adventure of The Further Adventures of the Star Wanderer

The Pitch

After years of television and indie film directing, it looked like Will Stone had finally gotten his break. His agent had called him about taking a meeting with Metamount Pictures, the legendary Hollywood studio known for its mega-blockbusters. Although Will didn't have much to go on other than the concept was low and the budget high, he felt that he could work with that.

But this. He wasn't quite sure he could work with this.

"Let me get this straight. You want me to direct a reboot of a film franchise that hasn't even been released yet?" Will tried to be respectful, as the executives sitting across from him in the small conference room were two of the most important men in Hollywood.

"Yes!" The first executive replied. He was short, bald, and thin, and thanks to too many facelifts his eyebrows were permanently raised in surprise.

"It is highly anticipated," the second executive added. He was older, and his face looked like one of those wrinkly dogs from China. The lines around his mouth seemed to make him look like he was smiling even when he wasn't. Will had been told they were named Murphy and Gwynn, but he didn't know which was which, and no one else seemed to really know either.

Will decided to just go with it, the prospect of a big payday overcoming his desire to politely decline their ridiculous idea. "So when will the first film be released?"

"It's a franchise, not a film, Mister Stone," said the first executive.

The second executive nodded. "A franchise."

After closing his eyes and taking a breath, Will corrected himself: "So when will the franchise be released?"

"Well," the first executive paused and then looked at the second executive, "the script hasn't been written yet."

"Ah, I see." Will did his best to enjoy the absurdity of the request but felt annoyed instead. "So how am I to remake this film—sorry, franchise—without knowing what the original was about?"

The first executive frowned, his facelift making him look like he was surprised to be frowning. "Not a remake, Mister Stone. A reboot."

"Yes, a reboot," the second executive added, all smiles. "You know, take the concept and then bring your unique style to the resulting film."

Will wasn't quite sure where this could possibly go next, so he decided to do his best to at least clarify how big his own role would be. "But isn't the reboot part of the franchise, too? So will

I be working on more than just directing the one film?" Will was thinking producer credits, but a string of big money sequels to direct wasn't a bad scenario either.

The first executive frowned. "I'm sorry if we weren't clear. You're just to work on the one film. The franchise is bigger than the reboot."

The second executive piped in. "The franchise is bigger than all of us."

"Yes, all of us," the first executive added, nodding.

Will tried to think of the request in Hollywood terms, which generally meant tossing reality aside.

He'd be making a film that probably wouldn't be released for years. There were plenty of examples of those. He'd also be rebooting a franchise. There were plenty examples of those, too. Sure, the timing was a bit ambitious—giving the greenlight on a reboot before the original franchise had even gotten its legs under it—but everything seemed to move faster in Hollywood these days.

The first executive must have sensed that Will was unsure, as he added, "The budget is two-hundred million dollars."

Will replied "yes" so quickly the second executive didn't even have time to comment.

Preproduction

It took three bourbons, two beers, and a Baywatch marathon for Will to clear his mind enough to grasp the reality that he was now required to actually write and direct The Further Adventures of the Star Wanderer. At least the money was also real. His agent had sent him a bottle of very expensive champagne and a note that said simply, "Thank you for not being an idiot."

The biggest problem was that he wasn't exactly sure what he was rebooting. The notes from the studio executives on The Star Wanderer were so vague as to be useless. They looked like a patchwork quilt of Firefly, Star Wars, Star Trek, and a dash of Battlestar Galactica. He had requested a script, but thus far all he'd been sent were bottles of wine with supportive notes from the studio.

On a lark and more than a little drunk, Will decided to just take the first act of Star Wars, add in some Star Trek in the second act, and then conclude with his version of Firefly. The characters would wander the galaxy for work after some kind of rebel/imperial battle that ended when the noble captain of an expeditionary ship discovers an advanced race that brought peace. He couldn't figure out how to get Battlestar Galactica shoehorned in, so he just left it out.

He sent the script to Metamount studios, assuming that they would finally send him the script of The Star Wanderer. As expected, he was called into the studio executives' office the next day. His agent said they were angry, but Will figured that after all they put him through, they'd understand him tossing them a joke script.

"I'm sorry; I'm not sure I understand," Will replied, staring at the two executives, anger visible on their faces. The first one looked surprised that he was angry. The other one looked happy he was angry.

"We asked for a reboot, Mister Stone!" The first executive

stabbed his finger on the script. "This is a copy of the plot of The Star Wanderer!"

"We expected daring, Mister Stone. We expected creativity, Mister Stone." The second executive sighed. "Not a rehash like this."

"Now, now," the first executive said to the second executive. "As this is a private conversation and we're all friends, I do think it is fair to say that this is actually a much better script than the one we have for The Star Wanderer."

"Indeed," said the second executive. "But it is still a rehash!"

"Wait a second," Will tried to grasp what he was hearing. "You mean this is the plot of The Star Wanderer?"

The second executive's smile wavered. "Don't play coy with us, Mister Stone. We're not sure how you got a copy of the script." He shot a glance at the first executive, who looked surprised at the implication of his involvement. "We've been very diligent about keeping that under wraps, but it's clear you know."

Will didn't like hearing that he was copying someone else, and the fact that he was seen as copying something so obviously awful made it even worse. He started to stand up to leave when the first executive held up his hands and blurted out, "Now, now, Mister Stone. This is certainly fixable. We just want you to not be so blatant in your reboot. As my esteemed partner said: Be daring! Be creative! Maybe add a lost colony drifting through space or something."

"Or pirates. Everyone likes pirates."

"Yes, pirates are good!"

"Reboot, not remake!" the second executive added.

Will slid back into his chair and muttered, "But the first movie hasn't even been made yet."

"Exactly!" the first executive said.

"Dry powder!" the second executive said.

"Boot—"

"And then reboot!"

The first executive stood up. "It's the future of film-making, Mister Stone."

Shooting

Will had to hand it to Metamount Pictures. The budget on the film was enormous, and he was thoroughly enjoying the process. He was walking actors around green screens with the knowledge he'd have an insane post-production SFX budget. He was blowing up massive live sets that must have cost millions of dollars. And the catering budget was enormous.

He had also finally wrangled the script to a point where it was a vague mix of Star Trek, Star Wars, and Firefly without really being any of the three. He still couldn't fit in Battlestar Galactica, but the executives seemed okay with it.

It was at exactly this point of enjoying and accepting the odd position he had been put in when he was called back to the Metamount offices for an emergency meeting.

"We have problems, Mister Stone." The first executive had circles under his eyes, while the second executive looked older and more wrinkled, if that was possible. Will had been called into the corner office a few times during filming in his directing career, but it was usually over budget or behavior issues, neither of which seemed a concern here.

"I'm sorry, is there a problem with the movie?"

The second executive pinched his nose with his fingers, and replied, "Indeed there is, which is why we need your help."

"Excuse me?"

"Yes, the script for The Star Wanderer was rejected by the star of the franchise, and I don't mean to tell you what that means, do I, Mister Stone?"

"No star. No franchise." The first executive added.

"Wait, is this about my film?"

The two executives looked at each other and then laughed. The first executive shook his head and replied, "Goodness, no, Mister Stone. Your film is going wonderfully, which is why we need your help. We love what we are seeing with The Further Adventures of the Star Wanderer, so we are hoping you would help us as a script consultant on The Star Wanderer."

"Script consultant?" They both nodded. "So The Star Wanderer hasn't even started filming yet?"

"Not yet, Mister Stone."

"But we have high hopes."

"It's a franchise."

"Which is why you're rebooting it."

"Exactly, rebooting it."

"But we could use your help on it."

"Indeed."

Will surprised himself by considering the offer. He had somehow become quite fond of the franchise, or at least his reboot of it. So he wanted it to start well. Still, he was working long hours already. "I'm not sure. I'm rather busy with this film."

"We'll give you points on the back end," the first executive replied.

"Back ends are nice," the second executive added.

By then the two voices had kind of blended into one, but the comment about points caught Stone's attention. For the second time in the Metamount Pictures development offices he uttered the words, "I'll do it."

He spent that night working on the script of The Star Wanderer while blocking scenes for the next day's shoot of The Further Adventures of The Star Wanderer. It took the same amount of beer but a few more bourbons for him to make it through.

Post Production

There was still no release date for his film, but then again there was no release date for The Star Wanderer yet, either. Will was only a few days from turning in the movie, and it made him sad. The actors were great. The special effects were groundbreaking, and the movie was something he felt proud of. He had taken the iconic elements of some of the most familiar science fiction staples and added his own touch of humanity, pathos, and humor. He would never say it publicly, but he felt that he had somehow turned mass-market schlock into art.

It was at this point that he was once again called into the Metamount Development office.

There was a bottle of champagne front and center on the conference room table, so Will knew that this was finally going to be a good meeting. The studio executives were relatively quiet about the dailies, but the final print had wowed everyone. Perhaps this was the meeting when they would announce a date for The Star Wanderer. Then his film would be released, what, six months later?

"First of all, congratulations on your film, Mister Stone. We absolutely love it."

"Love it."

"Thank you. I have to admit that I'm rather proud of the whole thing." Will leaned back and stretched his legs. He hadn't been this relaxed in a studio office in a long time.

The first executive stood up and walked around the conference table and sat on the edge. "There has, however, been one change." Stone looked at the second executive who didn't add his customary commentary. He just nodded. "We've decided not to release The Star Wanderer."

Will pulled himself up in his chair. "Wait a second. You're not going to release the movie that my movie is going to reboot?"

The second executive waved his finger. "No, no, no. You're rebooting the franchise."

"Yes, a franchise is bigger than a movie," the first executive added.

Will looked from one executive to the other. He was getting angry. He had played their stupid game, idiotic as it seemed, and finished with a damn good movie. Now, everything seemed doomed. "You do realize that I added references to the previous movie in The Further Adventures of the Star Wanderer?" Will had used his work with the first movie's script to subtly set up things in his movie. They were the kind of details that hardcore fans latched on to. As he filmed, he saw them as fortuitous. Now they were fundamental problems. In fact, at least one of them left a glaring plot hole. "There are key pieces that won't even work without the first movie!"

"Calm down, Mister Stone," the first executive reached for the champagne. "There is opportunity in change!"

"Opportunity." The second executive nodded.

"The buzz around The Star Wanderer is so great that it has exceeded even our expectations. We have coverage on every major scifi site on the Internet. There have been interviews with the director everywhere. The stars have become staples at cons. Do you know what cosplay is, Mister Stone?" Will nodded. "Well, there was more Star Wanderer cosplay at the recent San Diego Comicon than for Firefly."

"Firefly is a massive cult hit," the second executive helpfully added.

"So you can be sure that most people will already know the story." Will wasn't sure of that, but before he could reply, the first executive started to fiddle with the top of the champagne bottle as he continued. "In short, Mister Stone, the buzz around The Star Wanderer is so great that we are certain that actually releasing the movie will lead to disappointment."

The second executive stood up, nodding. "Disappointment is not good for a franchise."

The cork on the bottle of champagne popped, and the first executive held up the bottle. "So we're going straight to reboot!"

"Genius!" the second executive added as the first executive filled up the glasses with champagne. Will took his glass and finally realized he had to get out of Hollywood.

The idea actually made sense to him.

The Past Within

JAKE KERR
ON "THE PAST WITHIN"

Time travel stories will always be popular for the simple reason that all of us, at one point or another, have wished that we could go back and change the past or, at the very least, lived in it. But there is an intermediary step for those that travel back in time that is often missed—the awareness of the past as it actually was and the impact this has on the time traveler. In time travel stories, the past is a place that we change, not a place that changes us.

Even contemplation of the past is couched not in what it can teach us, but what our contemporary knowledge could bring to bear. The adage of "If I had only known then what I know now" is a perfect illustration of this. No one says "If I could only know now what I had known then."

But what if a sudden knowledge of the past actually changes who we are now? What if our memories have betrayed us or hidden from us things that would change how we are today? This important aspect of "time travel," so rarely explored, will be the subject of a novel I release in 2017. It explores how a woman doesn't actually go back in time but is able to go back through the deceptive depths of her memories, to see life as it actually was, not as it was remembered. What she discovers changes her entire life.

The story you are about to read is set in that same exact world, and it introduces the concept I will explore in my novel. Re-living a memory—something that sounds unremarkable—turns out to be life-changing in what it teaches about life today...

While the doctor tapped on a keyboard, Jasper Hill did his best to focus on the details of his wedding reception. *If I don't focus, I won't see her.* Sixty years hadn't dimmed his memory, but the medicinal smell in the room and the itchy skull implants were distracting. He reached up and touched one of the countless small metal bolts.

"You must focus, Mister Hill, or the memory retrieval will be incomplete and your experience will be compromised." He was having a hard time remembering the dessert they had served as the doctor's voice came from behind him. *Would that matter?* He was worried that if he forgot the dessert he'd forget her face.

"Relax, Mister Hill," the doctor's voice was soothing this time, rather than stern. "You're doing fine. Just don't let your mind wander."

Jasper dropped his hands to the chair and sat on them. This was his only chance to spend any extended time with his late wife Ruth, and he didn't want to blow it. *Crème Brulee, that was it.* It had been Ruth's favorite, and she wanted it served alongside the wedding cake.

In their preliminary scan, the doctors had identified his wedding day as the longest uninterrupted memory that Jasper had of his wife. He was able to recall without any aid many of the details, from his getting ready in his apartment to his arrival at the church to their own private moments late into the night. Now they were mapping his brain as he did his best to remember the day from beginning to end.

It would be the third and final step where he would finally be able to experience the day with Ruth again, complete with all of his senses. He would feel her lips against his. He would smell her hair. He would see her in her wedding dress. And her smile. He would see her smile.

"That's it. The markers are very clear now."

The wedding was sixty years ago, and Jasper hadn't seen Ruth in over fifteen. Now, thanks to Memory Experiences, he could finally spend some time with her again. The procedure had practically drained his retirement funds and was still labeled experimental, but Jasper didn't care. Spending time with Ruth again would be the last big gift he gave himself in his life.

Jasper had only one concern. He had caught his wife kissing an ex-boyfriend during the reception. No matter how hard he strained to remember, the aftermath was a blur. He didn't remember being angry. He didn't remember an argument. He didn't remember it ruining the wedding. All he could remember was a nagging feeling of doubt that lasted well into the first few years of their marriage.

Experience had taught him that what was a major thing when he was younger was something minor later in life, but he had to admit that the unknown scared him. What if he had buried the real, painful memory? What if he was about to re-live a day where his beloved Ruth really did betray him?

Still, the opportunity was just too great. He pushed the concern aside and thought of what he would see and feel when the doctors reconfigured his brain and sent him back. As they explained it to Jasper, he would be re-experiencing his wedding, only as the man who had been with her for decades.

"That's enough for today." The doctor started removing wires from his skull. "How you feeling?"

"Pretty good. I don't get the nausea any more."

"Fantastic. Your brain is getting used to having its neural connections redirected." The doctor placed a cap on Jasper's head, covering the small metal studs that protruded from across his skull in a dense pattern.

"Are we done with the mapping?"

"You tell me. How far did we get?"

"Dessert. We had crème brulee."

The doctor laughed. "Not wedding cake?"

"In addition to wedding cake."

"So, we still have ways to go. You remember the dances and the goodbyes, correct?"

"Yes," Jasper smiled as he remembered.

"Good. Then we should do at least another session, maybe two." The doctor sat down in a chair next to Jasper. "I assume we won't stop before the end of your wedding night?"

"If you're asking me if I remember everything until I fell asleep, I do. There's no reason to cut things short." He didn't say anything more, and the doctor didn't ask.

The next mapping session took him through to the end of the reception. It was mostly a blur, but the doctor said that was okay. They just needed to make sure they had neural connections in the area of his cerebral cortex where the memory lay. Once they started the process there would be a domino effect--the memories retained their initial connections and would flow from one to another. That he couldn't do it consciously wasn't a problem. Sometimes there were broken connections, but that's why they went through the in-depth mapping process--to reinforce the process with as many markers as possible along his cerebral cortex.

The final mapping session turned out to be difficult. Jasper felt he knew exactly how his and Ruth's wedding night went, from the moment he undid each of the countless buttons down the back of her dress, pausing each time to kiss the newly revealed skin, to the moment he fell asleep with his arms around her. He was wrong.

"Mister Hill, you need to be honest with me, please." Frustration filled the doctor's voice. "If you don't remember what happened it's fine. I just need you to remember what you can. Don't force it. This is the third time your mind has drifted from the hippocampus to the neocortex."

"I am not making up my wedding night!" Jasper had said the same thing twice already.

"I'm not saying you did, Mister Hill. I'm saying that you are embellishing things. It doesn't have to be with your actions. It can be you suddenly focusing on a detail that didn't exist or some words that weren't actually spoken." Jasper didn't say anything. "Just breeze through the evening. Don't focus on details. Trust me that you'll be able to experience it in a few weeks--you don't need to experience it now."

Jasper didn't tell the doctor, but he was becoming increasingly worried that something truly bad did happen, and that he had buried the memory. Still, he didn't live the life he did just to give up. So he tried his best, and they finished two hours later.

It turned out that there was one additional step before the Experience: an exit interview. It was the easiest part of the whole process. He didn't even see a doctor.

Jasper was directed to a small room, a cubicle really, where a young man sat behind a desk with a computer. "Jasper Hill?" The man didn't look up.

"Yes, sir."

He typed on the keyboard and then turned to Jasper. "Mister Hill, do you understand that there are no guarantees in the Memory Experience process and that Memory Experiences, Limited, assumes no liability for the procedure?"

"Yes." He had signed countless forms to that effect already.

"Do you understand that we are creating an experimental feedback loop between your cerebral cortex and its assorted complex memory areas and the neural centers of your brain that encompass sensory processing. Centers which include smell, sight, touch, hearing, and taste, but that there are no guarantees that you will experience any of these?"

"I do."

"Do you understand that due to the unknown nature of your memories, some of which may have been hidden from your consciousness for clinical reasons by your own mind, that this process may cause physical brain damage, psychological damage, damage to your senses, or even death."

Jasper paused. He had read the words many times, but hearing them spoken was different. That he actually did have a buried memory that would drive him insane seemed possible. "Yes, I understand." He didn't care.

The man looked back at the screen and then continued, without looking at Jasper. "Mister Hill, do you understand that the Memory Experience cannot guarantee any part of the process?

Your memories may be incomplete. They may not match up with what you actually remember. You may even remember and experience nothing."

Jasper sighed. By now he just wanted to get everything over with and see Ruth. "I understand."

"Finally, Mister Hill, you do understand that there are no refunds, no matter whether you experience what you hope for or not?"

"Yes. Yes. Yes. My funds have already transferred, and I know I'm not getting them back."

The man looked up, smiled, and said, "Great. You're all set to go, Mister Hill. How does next week look for you?"

Jasper smiled. Ruth, I will see you soon.

Jasper had read everything he could about the Memory Experience process, and nearly every comment repeated the same frustrating thing--I can't describe it. You just have to experience it. Now Jasper understood why.

As he stood in his old apartment bathroom getting ready for his wedding, everything he focused on was bright and sharp and detailed--yet the edge of his vision was just a bit vague, a bit blurry, a bit insubstantial. It was not at all like reality. He had no peripheral vision.

It was a small price to pay. He felt young, and as he looked at himself in the mirror, he was young--but it was still him, the older him. He liked the thought of living life over again with the knowledge and experience of all his years.

He awoke in his past brushing his teeth. His immediate thought was to put the toothbrush down and look around, but although he tried to move his hands he kept brushing his teeth. Of course, I'm a passenger. I can't change my actions.

Knowing that he couldn't change his memories and reconciling it with his reality were two different things, however. Jasper did his best to treat the experience like watching a movie, but his senses kept betraying him. The mint of the toothpaste tingled in his mouth, but he couldn't rinse until his younger self was ready. He was used to brushing lightly due to his sensitive gums, but his younger self attacked his teeth like he was scrubbing marble with a steel brush. To make things worse, he couldn't even close his eyes to get his bearings. The feeling of living a life where he had no physical control was unsettling.

It was difficult, but Jasper did his best to adjust to the dichotomy. The most frustrating part was when he badly wanted to investigate something but his old self was focused on doing something else. His lack of peripheral vision exacerbated things. He wanted to look around his apartment, but his younger self was focused on getting ready for the wedding.

At the edge of the bathroom mirror, Jasper caught a glimpse of a guitar in the corner of his one-room apartment that he had forgotten ever owning. On the other side of the room was a Radiohead poster. He hated Radiohead. Why was that there? Everything was new and remarkable, yet vaguely familiar.

Jasper stared at his face as he shaved. He had plenty of photos and, of course, remembered how he had looked, but it still felt like looking at a stranger. The scar above his left eye that he received in the car crash ten years earlier was gone. His full head of dark brown hair was back. He felt taller, although he wasn't sure he was. His skin was smooth. He felt strong.

After another frustration in trying to look left while his younger self looked right, Jasper started to get the hang of things. He accepted and followed the original memory as much as possible.

He couldn't believe how great he looked in his tuxedo. He enjoyed his hands adjusting his collar, his smile in the mirror, his wink to himself--so many things forgotten. Each newly experienced memory brought him a surge of happiness.

Things only got better when Raj picked him up to head to the church. Raj was his best friend from graduate school and had died a few years after their wedding. He couldn't remember a single word from their conversation during the drive to the church, but it was all there. He hung on every long-forgotten comment.

"So, do you miss Mary, Kim, Belle, April, and--wait, I lost count of all the others."

"Shut up, Raj." They both laughed.

"What kind of guy dates a woman named Belle anyway? Was that your 'I'm a Disney prince' phase?"

"She was hot." Jasper thought back and couldn't remember her. He was a bit embarrassed by his younger self's response.

"Nice. You are getting married in about thirty minutes, you know." Raj shook his head in disapproval.

"You brought them all up!"

Raj slapped him on the shoulder. "Just screwing with you,

man. I knew that they were all passing through." Raj leaned forward. "The moment you met Ruth I knew you'd marry her."

Jasper wanted to hug Raj. Or squeeze his shoulder. Something. He missed him terribly at that moment. Raj was right, of course, but there was so much more behind his words that his younger self just plain missed. Raj was saying that they would remain friends, even with Ruth in the picture. And that's what had happened. But then he died, and the memories were all that remained. The conversation continued, but Jasper ached to tell his friend how much he meant to him.

But he couldn't.

His younger self was too self-absorbed, too caught up in the moment. He punched Raj in the arm and replied, "Thanks, man."

It wasn't nearly enough.

As bittersweet as it was, spending time with Raj was a true gift. He was frustrated he couldn't tell his friend more, but then he realized it was only a memory that he couldn't change. It really wasn't Raj. Still, it was hard.

He was hanging around the side entrance to the church when his mom walked up. The dissonance between his shock in seeing his mom--dead some thirty years now--and the nonchalant actions of his younger self was painful.

His mom said hello and came up to give him a hug, and his younger self's rather dismissive-sounding, "Oh, hi mom," made Jasper realize how hard experiencing his memories could be. The limousine with Raj was easy in comparison.

Jasper's dad had died several years before he met Ruth, and Jasper eventually learned how difficult it was for his mom to let go.

He was the only man left in her life. Over the coming years, she would come to lean on him and Ruth. They would become very close. But to his younger self his mom was just a distraction.

"Stop it, mom. You're going to wrinkle my tux!" His mother stepped back and the pain on her face was as clear as day. She was worried that she was going to lose him to Ruth. But all the things that he knew now meant nothing to him back then.

She smiled. "You two will be very happy together. I just know it." Jasper saw tears forming on her face, but his younger self seemed oblivious.

"Thanks, mom." Jasper smiled. "Remember, you're in the limo with Raj."

His younger self turned away as his mom replied, "I'll try not to cry during the wedding."

"It's okay if you do," and at last his younger self turned back to his mom with something like the deep love that Jasper felt. "Hopefully she'll be as good a wife and mom as you."

His mom kissed him on the cheek, whispered a thank you, and wandered off. Jasper watched her walk toward the front of the church and then turned away. His groomsmen were returning from some errand or another.

Jasper's heart ached. He wanted nothing more than to spend time with his mom. He willed his body to turn to her. He knew that the rest of the day would be busy, and he didn't know if he would have another quiet opportunity to be alone with her. He screamed at his younger self to run after his mom, to hug her again, to tell her how much he missed her, that he could never have been the man he was without her. There were so many things to say. But his younger self had moved on.

The doctors had told him to expect surprises, but this was so much worse. This was powerlessness. It was like watching someone drown while you held a rope that was too short to save them.

Jasper didn't know if he could handle much more. He relaxed as the wedding coordinator opened the door, smiled, and said, "It's time." He stopped fidgeting and walked in.

He had clear memories and dozens of photos of his wedding, so the experience was a delight in the way that the previous interactions were not. He couldn't stop staring as Ruth came down the aisle. It was so far the only time that he felt perfectly in sync with his younger self. Their shared heart raced with every one of Ruth's steps.

As the two of them stood holding hands and looking at each other, Jasper wanted time to stop. He took in everything about her. Her dark hair and eyes. The dimple on the side of her face that age had slowly hid but he knew was always there. She smiled, and Jasper started to cry.

He quickly wiped his eyes with his thumb and forefinger and looked away. Jasper wanted to look at Ruth some more but his younger self fidgeted and couldn't focus. Was he really this nervous?

As his younger self tossed glances around the room, Jasper enjoyed seeing people he hadn't seen in decades, people he had forgotten but was glad to see again. There was his Uncle Bill in his plaid suit. There was his undergrad roommate, stoned off his gourd. Was that Paul and Dave his childhood friends? He didn't even remember inviting them.

All too soon the minister pronounced them man and wife. "You may kiss the bride" was spoken, words that Jasper had waited to hear from the first day he had walked through the front doors of Memory Experiences. He looked Ruth in the eyes, leaned forward, and kissed her.

He remembered the kiss lasting forever when he was twenty-three, but it was painfully short now. He clung to the experience, the memory. The soft warmth as their lips touched. How her lipstick was slightly flavored cherry. The smile that formed before the kiss was even over. The way she stared in his eyes.

As they separated, he leaned forward and spoke to his wife for the first time in fifteen years, a whisper in her ear. Jasper didn't remember saying anything to Ruth at the altar, so he focused entirely on the moment.

"I can't wait to get you naked."

Jasper was stunned. Why would he say such a thing? She looked so beautiful, and the moment was full of romance and joy. He wondered if this was even a real memory. But as he thought of his younger self he knew it was true.

He turned away to face the guests, but Jasper had time to glance at Ruth's face. She was still, and he could see a slight frown. He wanted to throttle himself. The most important and romantic moment of his and Ruth's life together, and he thought saying that was a good idea? He felt embarrassed.

They held hands as they walked down the aisle. Jasper wouldn't have blamed Ruth for distancing herself from him at that moment, but her grip was strong, and as he glanced over at her amongst the well wishers, she had a bright smile on her face.

In the limo on the way to the reception, Jasper pushed his embarrassment aside. He was starting not to like his younger self, but sitting next to Ruth, resplendent in her gown, seemed to make everything better.

He reveled in the miracle of being with her again. She leaned her head against his shoulder, looked up, and they kissed. Each time she kissed him or brushed against him or touched him it made his heart beat faster. He stared at her. He laughed at her nervous jokes and smiled at her every movement. His decades-long love for her never lost its flame.

As they exited the limo, Ruth went off to the side to have her hair fixed. Jasper looked at her and thought back to the moment on the altar. How could he be so selfish, so vulgar? His younger self was an idiot. He was surrounded by his mother, Ruth, and Raj--and he squandered each moment.

Jasper was prepared to give his younger self the benefit of the doubt. After all, it was his wedding and nervousness was to be expected, but now he worried that these were symptoms of a bigger failing.

Maybe it wasn't the kiss with her former boyfriend that made their first few years so difficult. Maybe it was him. And the thought made Jasper love his wife all the more. She didn't marry the man he thought he was. She made the boy she married into that man.

Ruth returned and took his hand. He leaned over and kissed her. His younger self didn't say anything, but in his mind Jasper whispered, "Thank you."

He enjoyed the reception, but thoughts of Ruth's forthcoming kiss with her old boyfriend started to intrude. Was he going to be shocked by Ruth's behavior during the kiss like he was shocked by his own during the wedding? Maybe the kiss was one of longing or wistfulness, the kiss of someone fed up with the immaturity of her new husband. He couldn't remember, and he couldn't blame her.

His younger self seemed to mirror his tension. He got into a small argument with Ruth's sister over her standing too close during some photos. He didn't remember that. In the middle of Raj's emotional toast, Jasper threw a balled up napkin at him. He remembered that but had forgotten Ruth's glare and the disapproving murmurs after he did it.

The moment arrived. Jasper did everything he could to keep his younger self from leaving the seat for the restrooms, leading to that moment. But it did no good.

He didn't want to face Ruth kissing her old boyfriend because although he had accepted one sad reality--he was an immature selfish jerk when he was twenty-four, he did not want to face the possibility of another--that Ruth's kiss was a symbol of the regret she felt in marrying him.

As his younger self got up and moved across the room, Jasper calmed himself by focusing on the later part of his and Ruth's lives together. Everything worked out. This memory meant nothing. She stayed with him. Their life was wonderful.

Still, he was scared.

He walked through the door to the foyer, and there the two of them were, talking quietly. They stopped talking, and then the ex-boyfriend—Jasper couldn't even remember his name—grabbed Ruth by the shoulders, leaned in, kissed her lightly on the lips, and stepped back.

Jasper's heart was racing, and he felt his fists clench, but inside he smiled. His younger self was watching a different scene. The kiss was hardly proper at a wedding, but it wasn't a passionate kiss between two lovers either. It was a kiss goodbye from someone who didn't want to let go. Jasper felt sorry for the guy.

As Jasper started walking toward them, he looked at Ruth. She looked confused, but it was clear to him that she wasn't confused over her feelings but over how to react. Jasper laughed at himself. His clueless younger self clenched his fists again. He didn't even understand the reaction of his own wife.

She heard Jasper's footsteps and smiled as she caught his eyes. He remembered thinking that Ruth didn't know he saw the kiss, but re-experiencing the memory made it clear that there was no way she wouldn't have known he was there. That she didn't care illustrated how much she trusted him, while his response illustrated how he didn't deserve that trust.

"You didn't tell me you invited Paul!" Her voice was bright and happy and didn't contain a hint of guilt. The older Jasper knew there was no reason for her to feel guilty, but the younger Jasper was upset. His heart beat fast, and he put his hands in his pockets to stop them from shaking.

"I knew you were friends for a long time." He paused to stop his voice from shaking. Ruth didn't appear to notice. "I thought it would be nice for you to see him." Jasper's voice was cold and flat.

The words were a surprise. He didn't remember inviting Paul. Hell, he couldn't even remember Paul's name.

Jasper stopped in front of them, and Paul shook his hand. "You're a good man, Jasper. Ruth's a lucky girl."

There was a big smile on Ruth's face, but Jasper only nodded. He didn't say a word to Paul, but rather turned to Ruth. "I have to use the restroom, but we need to get back in. They're getting ready for the last few dances." He turned to Paul. "Paul," was all he said, nodding his head. He waited to use the restroom until Ruth had re-entered the ballroom.

The younger Jasper spent the rest of the night on edge. His younger self didn't know how to react to what he saw, so he barged ahead in some kind of sad attempt to prove to Ruth that she shouldn't be interested in anyone else. He clung to her, constantly whispered romantic things in her ear, and was overly polite to everyone. Jasper remembered feeling nothing but a vague tension at the time and, more than anything, a difficulty in enjoying himself.

Now, however, he experienced everything completely differently.

The physical actions were identical, but while the younger Jasper felt stress and unease, Jasper felt joy and love and exuberance.

During a slow dance, he whispered into Ruth's ear, "I don't ever want to let you go." He wasn't sure what his younger self meant, whether it was pathos or fear or something more positive, but to Jasper, it was exactly how he felt. As they separated, his eyes glanced away, but Jasper noticed that Ruth's eyes were wet with tears. He wondered if his younger self noticed.

Everything was a delight, and Ruth was a marvel of beauty and love. Eventually, Jasper forgot he was even experiencing the evening as his younger self. The memories and even the physical reactions transformed something immature and even ugly into something wonderful and joyous.

Ruth was actually with him, the older Jasper, not the clueless fearful younger one. Each protective embrace was actually one of love, not possessiveness. Each suspicious glance was one of adoration. Each word of love was given out of sincerity, not fear.

Each moment was his and Ruth's alone.

At one point Ruth and her sorority sisters danced together. He sat at the head table and watched as the young women finished laughing and falling all over themselves. Jasper smiled.

Ruth caught his eye and walked over. He shook his head as she sat down next to him. "Kind of embarrassing, that." His younger self laughed as he said it, relaxing for the first time since the kiss earlier in the evening.

She shrugged. "There are worse things in life than embarrassing yourself." She shoved against him with her shoulder and smiled. Once again Jasper's younger self missed the nuance, the undercurrent of meaning behind his wife's words. But he caught it. She knew exactly who she was marrying. She knew. He was young and impetuous and kind of embarrassing, but she loved him anyway.

Jasper looked her in the eyes and shook his head. "If you say so."

"I say so." She stood up. "Speaking of embarrassing yourself--" She walked a few feet and then looked back over her shoulder. "You want to dance?"

The wedding ended, and they made their way to the hotel. In the back of the limo, Jasper and Ruth kissed again. As she pulled away, he continued to hold her. She looked uncertain. He then pulled her in for a longer passionate kiss. Jasper could smell her perfume, taste a bit of cherry, and feel her soft lips and tongue.

As they slowly parted, he whispered in her ear, "You're the best thing that's ever happened to me."

She leaned forward and placed her lips so close to his ear that Jasper could feel her breath. His heart beat fast as she whispered, "I know," and she bounded backward laughing. He smiled and tried to slap her on her bottom, but the wedding dress got in the way, and his hand just ended up swatting lace and fabric.

In their honeymoon suite Jasper unbuttoned each of Ruth's buttons with a kiss. And as he later lay down to sleep he remembered his frustrating last session with the Memory Experiences doctor. He had said that he was not making up his wedding night. Despite his fear, Jasper knew it was perfect as it was.

He was right.

———————————

Jasper had a lingering headache the next day as he stood before Ruth's gravestone. He knelt down and rearranged the roses one more time. Reaching forward, his hand trembled as he lightly touched the words engraved in the marble under Ruth's name. Her Love Touched Us All.

Standing up, Jasper took a deep breath and looked around at the flowers, the grass, the blue sky, and his wife's name in the marble. "I remember," he whispered as he began the walk back to his car.

ABOUT THE AUTHOR

After fifteen years as a music industry journalist Jake Kerr's first published story, "The Old Equations," was nominated for the Nebula Award from the Science Fiction Writers of America and was shortlisted for the Theodore Sturgeon and StorySouth Million Writers awards. His stories have subsequently been published in magazines across the world, broadcast in multiple podcasts, and been published in multiple anthologies and year's best collections. He is the author of the Tommy Black and Guildmaster Thief fantasy series.

A graduate of Kenyon College, Kerr studied fiction under Ursula K. Le Guin and Peruvian playwright Alonso Alegria. He lives in Dallas, Texas, with his wife and three daughters.

www.jakekerr.com
@jakedfw

www.ingramcontent.com/pod-product-compliance
Lightning Source LLC
Chambersburg PA
CBHW060942180626
46817CB00004B/1675